John Pomeroy

The Scandinavian Ring

A novel. Part 3

John Pomeroy

The Scandinavian Ring
A novel. Part 3

ISBN/EAN: 9783337045944

Printed in Europe, USA, Canada, Australia, Japan

Cover: Foto ©Andreas Hilbeck / pixelio.de

More available books at **www.hansebooks.com**

THE SCANDINAVIAN RING.

A Novel.

BY

JOHN POMEROY,

AUTHOR OF 'GOLDEN PIPPIN,' 'HOME FROM INDIA,' ETC. ETC.

IN THREE VOLUMES.—VOL. III.

LONDON:

TINSLEY BROTHERS, 18, CATHERINE ST., STRAND.

1871.

CONTENTS OF VOL. III.

THE SCANDINAVIAN RING.

CHAPTER I.

RUDOLF AND BESSIE.

LEAVING Robert and his efforts for a time, for he went backwards and forwards more than once, and suffered distress and disappointment, we may follow Bessie, who lived for three years or more at the Morton Langdales, for Rudolf's fortunes were not of the brightest.

A country house full of visitors is very gay and cheerful: gentlemen go out to shoot, and leave the ladies for the whole day, which is quite natural, and only the foolish ones grumble, though at times we do hear of girls who dress in thick boots, and can fire a gun as well as their brother, or officer friends, and have no more compunction in bringing down a partridge or grouse than in plucking a flower.

One morning Mrs Morton Langdale and her sister, newly arrived from the Sister Isle, where her husband had been quartered, and whence he had come for the delights of September, Mrs the hostess and Mrs the guest sat in the breakfast parlour, after all the others had left.

'I cannot think,' said the latter, ' why you took a Danish governess, you who are so particular about accent.'

'I have tried so many, and either they have been too attractive or too ugly. I heard of Mademoiselle Brinkmann when she was with Lady Susan Golden, and I was assured by the Paris agent that her academical French was to be relied upon. I have not yet regretted our choice.'

'No, you have had this Dane a long time; is she good-looking?'

'Very; that is, in my eyes; but she keeps out of our way very much, and still goes to the Trulybridges when she can, and, I suppose, has some Danish friends to console her, for she is no trouble.'

'Is she expensive?' Mrs Brembridge asked.

'No, Laura, not at all. We give her a hundred a year, as we gave the other finishing governesses; but they all wanted so many extras. This lady asks for nothing but reasonable comfort.'

'She did not get that, I suspect, at the Duchess of Goldenisle's.'

'I have never heard; she does not tell us anything of that sort.'

'She is a paragon! Does she come into the drawing-room in the evenings?'

'Very seldom;—she prefers to have the evening to herself. She objects to spend her money in evening dress, I fancy, and the girls tell me she has letters to write in the evenings. It is that we like so much. The last governess we had was so over-dressed; she was absurd, and she used to challenge Henry to amuse her with écarté or chess.'

'Perhaps she thought she amused him.'

'Perhaps so, Laura; but she got him into bad habits. He used to fall asleep to avoid her; indeed, poor thing! she was very vain, and always sought to bring her accomplishments forward.'

'What did you do with her?'

'Sent her away, of course.'

'Perhaps Miss Brinkmann has fewer.'

'Oh no, even more; but she is of a quieter temperament, and seems satisfied with her lot.'

'Then she is in love,' said Mrs Brem-bridge, 'for I never knew a governess who was not seeking first for her own establishment in life, and then to get her pupils on.'

'She has not told me she is; but, Laura, the girls are so much improved, so nice and pleasant, I cannot think how she makes them so industrious, for Fairy was the idlest thing in the world, except Posy; besides, she never teases Henry, and is never in my way.'

' Was the other in your way ? '

' Always; we met on the stairs, or in the hall. If I wanted a quiet walk, she used to follow me; if I went to pay a visit, she officiously followed me too ; and in the evening, if I sat down to the piano to amuse Henry, she wanted to relieve me. She had no tact.'

' What an intolerable nuisance ! ' said the officer's wife, Laura. ' Did she get married from here, like her predecessor ? '

' No; she had too much manners. I think she put every one on his guard ! Poor woman ! Fancy Henry's face when she offered to read the *Times* aloud to him ! '

' What a pest ! '

'The climax was when she wished to relieve him of the task of reading prayers! He closed his near-sighted eyes at her, and took the book back from her hands without a word, but I could hear a titter from the servants ; and so we dismissed her speedily.'

'Has Miss Brinkmann tact?'

'Plenty, and pride too. She comes of an ancient race, and has the gift of seeing everything in its proper light. She has extraordinary discrimination, and never makes mistakes.'

'I want to see her, Helen.'

'Curb your curiosity. You will see her in time, and too much of Fairy and Posy, who are grown so tall, you will be frightened at them. They are both very nice with Miss Brinkmann, who came so evidently to be their governess and no more in the household, that we have quite a pleasant sensation of independence.'

'Then she is not a lady whose feelings

are always on the *qui vive*, and ready to be hurt?'

'Nothing can be further from her character. For a year together there is no variation: her temper is perfect. She never resents fancied injuries, or meets with slights or want of attention.'

'The study of governesses amuses me,' said Mrs Brembridge. 'I have met with such strange examples. Going from place to place I see a great deal of life; and I must say people seem to take a governess with very little consideration, and I have seen some treated very badly.'

'I assure you, Laura, I am without any prejudice; but I have suffered a good deal on their account. However, I am quite satisfied now. The girls are very happy; Miss Brinkmann does her duty, and takes her money, feeling she has earned it; and there is no fuss with her about the bread of servitude, as the other called it.'

'I hope it agrees with her, at any

rate,' said Mrs Brembridge, laughing.

'Yes, I think it does. She never complains, and that is one good thing with the girls, who are not fanciful. I believe the Danes never teaze with their ailments as the English do.'

'They do; every one this morning complained of something! I do not think they ever grumble in Ireland as they do in England.'

'No, Laura, I believe not.'

Mrs Morton Langdale had to leave her sister to attend to more ceremonious guests; and driving and other occupations took up the day. After dinner Mrs Brembridge, who had seen her lovely nieces, Fairy and Posy, began to look for the governess.

Bessie entered the room with her quiet, dignified manner, and took Mrs Brembridge by surprise,—she was so different from any governess she had yet seen. Her beautiful figure, rounded and supple; her fair complexion and hazel eyes, made her attractive as a person; but there was something quite entrancing when she spoke.

'I came this evening,' Bessie said to Mrs Langdale, with a graceful acknowledgment of her as she went towards where she sat, 'for I thought you might wish to hear your daughters play or sing.'

Mrs Brembridge saw her sister, and heard 'Thank you' accompany her looks of pleasure, as if Bessie were conferring a favour, which it turned out to be; for when the three, any or all of them, sang or played, it was a high gratification to the guests. 'Music well chosen and well performed,' was the verdict.

'What a charming person Miss Brinkmann is,' said old Sir Thomas Ware next morning. 'I never met any Danes except at Florence, where a family of them dined at the Nuova Yorka hotel; but they all had flat faces and ugly noses!'

'So you expected our Dane to have an ugly nose,' said the host.

'I believe I did; and you know the Florentine fashion of eating figs and slices of Bologna sausage, as one of the courses at dinner. I always associated Danes with Bologna sausage, in honour of those people.'

'I have met some pleasant Danes,' said another gentleman.

'And I met one very agreeable Dane at the Baths of Lucca,' Sir Thomas Ware continued; 'but he was broad and flat-faced, and very much given to figs and sausages!'

'Odd specimens do get abroad from every country,' Major Brembridge remarked. 'When I first went to Ireland I was astonished at the people, so different from the specimens I had seen; and I felt disappointed that all the men were not named "Pat," and all the women "Biddy."'

'Oh, Cyril,' said his wife, 'do leave

Ireland alone. When once that subject of prejudices takes part, conversation never knows where to restrain itself.'

'What new turn have you taken, Laura?'

'A prudential one,—namely, to let Ireland alone.'

'Why, Laura, what a change!'

'Yes, Henry, I am changed. Cyril, put down your eye-glass. At the first acquaintance with Ireland I took up the cudgels in her behalf. I took up all her grievances; talked about her, wrote about her; brought hot water and hornets' nests about myself, and—'

'And did no good, I suppose?'

'None, Sir Thomas,' the lady said.

'You were always inclined to be Quixotic about Ireland, too, Brembridge,' said Sir Thomas Ware. 'What are your notions now?'

'My wife has exploded all my theories for me.'

'And I,' said the lady, 'have given the whole thing up, as the yacht-man in *Punch* says.'

'Well, Laura, have you and Cyril come to reason?'

'We have, Henry. I am not going to fight for Ireland any more. She has not come up to my expectations; she has disappointed me. Cyril, don't laugh; I am not going to talk any more about it.'

'Nor fight?'

'Let those who make their battles be the only ones to fight,' said the lady. I mean to go in for Denmark now. Helen, may I have Miss Brinkmann, and Fairy, and Posy, and the pony-carriage?'

'*And* welcome,' said the hostess, as she rose from the breakfast-table, and the guests dispersed.

Miss Brinkmann's reasons for being contented lay in her pocket,—Rudolf's letters.

'My own,' said the last, 'I am longing

to meet you again. Major and Mrs Brembridge little think how I envy them. It is the joy and wine of life, Bessie, to think of you; and I dare say when Brembridge's leave is over I shall hear him speak of you. His wife is a lively, clever woman. No news of my father. I am lonely and very much out of spirits. This little note of love, my darling, is to enclose Bob's last. The dear fellow! It is a shame he is kept out of money: I cannot tell how much I feel for him. Your own   RUDOLF.'

Robert's letter enclosed said—

'Kiel harbour, on board the "Panurge."

'DEAR RUDOLF,

'The evergreen oaks, the rolling sand-bluffs, all the flat pastures, and the thousand windmills tell me I am here again; but I have a dead, *blunt* sort of feeling;—I am here again for nothing. Bessie would like to see the tulips,—they seem

" extra" good this year. Large Mosaic patterns are formed of them; the richness is surprising. I was always fond of tulips; when a child, I used to stand over them in the old St Nicholas garden; and then look up to the pearls in the tall Crown Imperials, of which our mother was so excellent a cultivator.

' The finest variety of roses have found their way out here now. I wish things were settled; I could be so happy anywhere now. I am tired of knocking about, and very tired of poverty. I cannot feel certain of anything. I wanted to get here; now, already, I have lost hope, and the Magnusens are as much at a loss as we are. Certainly Thorwaldsen's little Iceland is a queer island. Hecla was in good humour, and the springs in excellent condition; but all the herrings in the Sound will not bring contentment, as old Nikel says. Love to Bessie when you write. The farms and neat hedges have a very

English look. It will be the old story, I
know, whether I write from Jutland,
Copenhagen, or Kiel. Again, God bless
you, old fellow.

‘ Bob.’

Over and over again Bessie would read
the packets of Rudolf's letters. He was
very fond of her, and, moreover, had the
gift of expressing his feelings on paper,
which many want ; and thus to them
credit is not given for that depth and
warmth which they deserve.

Rows of shelves, filled with French,
German, and Italian volumes, were on one
side of Bessie's room at the Morton Langdales, the school-room of Fairy and Posy,
and great globes, which appear to be in-
dispensable to girls' education, though
boys always do without, were in loose
green baize covers in two corners, maps
and charts, and ideal landscapes were sus-
pended on the walls, and these all gave

place to prettier and newer adornments, which occupied little tables, and gave the room a home-like look.

Bessie had learned a great deal since she left the Duchess of Goldenisle's; and knew that globes and routine did not lay the foundation of human happiness. She had flowers and plants for her Fairy and Posy; and they were full of hope, and very different from poor Alice, or even Lady Susan Golden. She had struck for a carpet, and told Mrs Morton Langdale that bad fires and neglected cold would lay the seed of consumption; so having once mentioned the death of Lady Alice, Bessie had every requisite at discretion.

Bessie had gained experience, and had come to feel that people who could afford to educate their daughters with all the accomplishments of modern times should allow a certain sum for their bodily comfort; so the Miss Morton Langdales had good fires, and proper paint-boxes, and easels for their drawing, and such requisites as health and position demanded.

Even dark green curtains were hung in the apartment in which the fair-haired governess spent most of her time, and it was from there she wrote words to sustain and comfort Rudolf.

'You must let me send you the fifty pounds which I now have,' she said; 'it will make you a little more free. I cannot bear to think of you and Robert, with no money coming in, and I know you cannot live on your pay. I have seen the Major and Mrs Brembridge you mention, and like them; and "Cyril" and "Laura" get on well together. Oh, Rudolf, if Robert could restore your amulet! for you see I have fallen into the superstition, and believe that our ill-fortune dates from its loss. If it were restored, we, Rudolf, could be going about together, like Cyril and Laura! Do not fancy I am complaining; far from it. I have become a woman of experience, and have learned to wait. After the 25th of next month I shall be looking for your change : if you come to England, we can meet. Time will bring reward for all our self-denial, and, I trust, with good news of Robert.'

But in another ten days the fond pair had to give up the little hope concerning the 25th, for Rudolf then said—

'My darling, I can scarcely believe it, as I can hardly bear to think of it. We are not to leave Ireland after all, and my regret is extreme, for our meeting must be postponed *sine die*. It cannot be helped : keep up your spirits, dearest. I trust to your love to keep up mine ; but it is very hard to bear. Even one hour with you would relieve me. All the fellows are depressed; for the Pigeon-house Fort is not lively, and the hospitality of Ireland is a thing of the past—gone like a spent meteor. They used to flash it over the vision of a regiment, and dazzle it with hopes. For my part, it is indifferent. I only want one society. I mean yours. I have reports, and all sorts of writing to do, so I must go to it; but I am only doing my duty in writing first to the woman whom I have chosen before the whole world. Dear Bessie, when am I to proclaim you as my wife in the face of all people ?'

It takes a good deal of courage for a man to leave his beloved anywhere or at any time. It tries his temper, and his heart is apt to discover little tendencies to jealousy which were never pre-supposed to exist; and when Rudolf found he was not to get away from Dublin for a long time, he took a very decided hatred to the place, and indulged in more prejudices towards Ireland and the Irish than were necessary.

He had to listen to Major Brembridge's observations of all sorts with what patience he could bring to bear, for he had enjoyed his leave; but Rudolf was on the point of combustion when he spoke of a lovely, fair-haired Danish governess, whom he had met in a country-house, to which he had gone for some shooting. He spoke of her fine figure and musical talents on several occasions, and once, when abundant hair had become the topic under discussion, he instanced 'that fair Danish girl'; and Rudolf bit his moustache with a pang of hidden jealousy and love that it was hard for him to keep beneath the surface.

Just at the moment, however, when Rudolf thought that if Major Brembridge said another word of Bessie he must have shot him, a Miss St Lawrence was luckily mentioned, who had been the belle at a ball at the Dublin Mansion House, and her beauties being the exact opposite of Bessie's, it was very easy to keep the ball rolling in her direction, and one or two fortunate touches did so, and Rudolf's spirits had time to resume their balance.

If he experienced misery in hearing too much said of Bessie, she had the reverse misery of hearing almost nothing of her beloved for a long time. He was gone to Ireland; and to her it was far more effective in creating the feeling of distance between them than if he were gone to the North Pole: for there she knew he must have waited for the breaking up of the ice, or something over which neither the one nor the other could exercise the least control. Ireland seemed to her an unknown country; she had never met with people who had been there but once, and they had a Dublin accent, and were not *créme de la créme*. These persons she had seen at Dover, when she spent the short time there with Lady Alice, her pupil, now gone with the past.

Rudolf did not, for her sake, write often. He felt that it might be better for her that he should not, and, unfortunately, denied himself a pleasure which would have been very great, and also very good for both of them.

Bessie kept his letters in her pocket, and read and re-read them, and longed for more with a true womanly yearning, and when they came she was radiant and joyous.

Day followed day. Christmas came, snowy and cold. Posy was taken away with her mother to pay a Christmas visit to some relations. Fairy devoted herself to her brother in his holidays,—he never once entered the school-room. Bessie had her work and her books there to herself; she wrote long letters to her Rudolf, but kept them as a sort of journal very long before she posted them. Something of a new propriety seized her with regard to Dublin. She did not like her letters to go through stranger hands. At Portsmouth she had written to him daily: she felt that there, or in college-rooms, a man's correspondence came to him directly, but at the

Pigeon-house Fort it all seemed different, and a vague doubt annoyed her—that the Pigeon-house Fort, being somewhere outside Dublin, the postal regulations might be in every way different, and her letters might be submitted to the Lord-lieutenant himself, who might have the handling of all documents in these troubled times, and that her epistle to Rudolf would be looked on as an innocent and unimportant matter, and be made over to him at any time suited to official convenience.

In one of her rare letters she told him something of this, and how much she wished he were in England; then she gave an account of her time of relaxation,—how Posy was gone, and was admired, and how proud she felt of her attainments; then how Fairy had become strong and able to go out, even in the snow, with her brother and his friends; that they were at that instant gone out with a lantern to see if the ice would be likely to bear for skating to-morrow; that the servants were out in the court-yard enjoying a good game at snow-balling. She added—

'I never mean to put on my skates again till I am with you; I wish no one to help me but you, and a hand must be near for skating. It is the same reason that makes me refuse to dance,—no one shall touch my hand or place his arm where Rudolf's was last time we danced together.'

Rudolf wrote after Christmastide was over—

'We have been kept busy night and day, not as people in England imagine, with balls and gaiety, the nominal fate of officers stationed in Ireland. If you had seen the fellows who landed at Kingstown the other day from the "Orontes," you would have pitied them.

'George Harris wrote a song on the occasion, beginning, "The Orontes steamer landed me upon the Irish coast." You know I am not good at remembering poetry, but this has been "a hit," and has gone the rounds already, for it gives a ludicrous picture of reality, as opposed to anticipation.'

Another letter of Rudolf's said—

'The feeling of uncertainty in which we live makes Ireland quite different from any other quarters. It is hard work to go on thus. There is a want of confidence instilled everywhere, which I suppose serves to keep us on the *qui vive*. I find it creeps into all society; it is absurd to see even young ladies in the upper classes utterly without sincerity. As I care for none of them, and have no claim upon nor connection with Ireland, perhaps I see these things more plainly than others do. I also having for my standard candour and purity in you, cannot see these girls act with entire contempt of truth and honour without surprise.

'By the way, a great barter goes on of foreign postage stamps. Get Helga to send

me all the Danish and Norwegian out,
which will tend to my popularity. You
tell me traits of character, my Bessie, but
all redounding to the good of your friends.
What do you think of a little occurrence
which passed under my eyes last week?
Two of us were invited to a country-
house, where a wedding had taken place.
Poultry of some uncommon sort appeared to be the *specialité* of the family,
and at the breakfast-table, on the morning
after the ball, some eggs of a dark colour
led to discussion.

'"Miss Edith," said a gentleman guest,
"may I beg for half-a-dozen eggs?" He
said of what kind, but it sounded like Man-
dalixy to me.

'"Oh, certainly, Sir James," was the
smiling reply.

'Another gentleman put in for some
also, and to him she also promised them in
the most ingenuous manner. I could see
the lady mamma was not gratified at her

daughter's liberality, nor was I prepared
for the girl's treachery.

'After these gentlemen had moved away,
I was yet lingering over the day's papers,
when the mother said,

' " Edith, you were wrong to promise all
those eggs; I thought we were to have the
prize at the Prince of Wales's show."

' " So we shall, mamma."

' " But it is rash to give so many,
Edith."

' " I do not mean them to hatch," said
the young lady candidly and coolly.

' " How so, Edith ? "

' " Oh, mamma, I shall give them a dip
in boiling water, then they will never come
to anything."

'She did not lower her voice, nor did the
mother express surprise, so I conclude the
young lady has been brought up devoid of
honour, which, I agree with you, ought to
be expected in a woman as much as in
a man; but girls in Ireland appear

to have neither honour nor generosity.

'We had an amusing and ludicrous adventure driving back. The other fellow who was invited with me was the owner of the dog-cart, but we took my servant, the Portsmouth man, " Mitts," of whom you have heard. He sat behind.

'George Harris had a great deal to say to every one at parting, and began to tell me all his ball-room adventures as soon as we were off. Within a couple of miles of Dublin he pulled up to give a friend of his a lift beside " Mitts." Now, this Dublin friend was well used to cars, but not to George's fast trotting mare, and English springs, I suppose, astonished him. George related all sorts of things, and we went at a fine pace. I heard " Mitts " say something, but George laughed at his own story, and I joined him, never thinking of our " friend of Eblana," as Harris calls him, till I felt "Mitts" touch me on my back, unable to call attention otherwise. He said in a plaintive tone,

' " Oh, dear! oh, dear! the gent's fell off."

' It was even so. Harris looked behind. There was our " friend of Eblana" running hard after us. He took it good-temperedly enough, and again seated himself beside " Mitts." George Harris never said another word about ball or supper, but spent the rest of the time in suppressed laughter, till we got back to our quarters, where we made it up to our friend, More Hibernico, with " a glass." '

CHAPTER II.

FAIRY AND POSY.

M̲RS MORTON LANGDALE came back before the Christmas vacation was over, and a fine season of frolic followed in order to wind up the young people's holidays in the most delightful manner. Charades, or rather private theatricals—for they were worthy of the name—two balls, and excellent skating, thanks to the severity of the cold, for every lake and river became available for amusement. Young ladies looked lovely in the gay bright petticoats and sealskin jackets, the elders in velvet and sable.

All that Morton Langdale could do

was done, and Bessie was cheerful, and her pupils did her infinite credit. She heard of Rudolf in a very pleasant manner, for Mrs Morton Langdale read her sister's letters aloud at breakfast-time, and he was frequently mentioned. Mrs Brembridge had also opened her eyes to the state of things present in Ireland, and ceased to expect things impossible, such as union, where it cannot come, or peace, where there is no love.

'They tell me that orange and green unite,' she said, 'but I say nothing, and it only makes me think of rows of yellow crocuses growing on the grass where they have no business to be, but rather planted in nice orderly tufts in the flower-borders, so I never see the striped yellow and green without some foolish observation on colour, which prevents political discussion; for instance, "blue and yellow would make green, but yellow and green do not go well;" then they think I am a fool and *voilà tout!* I have given the whole thing up, and put in my time as peaceably as I can, in a country for which I have no longer interest, and amongst people for whom I make no further effort to get up friendship. We are English, and so are victims of prejudice, and now that my eyes, as Cyril says, are open, I can see and judge clearly. I used to think it was only that English people were prejudiced against Ireland, I now see that prejudice is ten times stronger on the Irish side against the English.

' Our new neighbourhood is very gay, at least I am told so. I have not seen this, and I must say the sort of town and people appear to preclude such a possibility.

' Captain Beaumont and our friend George Harris arrived last night. They do not seem to be inspired with much hope as to the change. Captain Beaumont is the handsomest man (next to Cyril) in my eyes, and George Harris has

the most fun! The town of Newbridge
is most detestable, but it has good bar-
racks, Cyril says, though beyond a canal
and wharves, and all sorts of nasty places,
I expect fever and small-pox ought to be
looked for as far as I can judge, though,
thank God, Ireland does escape in some
miraculous manner even when she appears
to court such scourges. The climate must
be healthy to a great degree: nobody ever
seems to mind anything; the canal floods
the streets and runs into the cellars, and
the dirt is not carted away; everything
goes on in a "happy-go-lucky" sort of
manner, and no one is the worse.

' We have what are said to be the best
lodgings in Newbridge,—they are over a
china shop, and the owner is the wife of a
bootmaker, who has another shop opposite.
A confectioner lives next door to us who
has been in the habit of providing lunch-
eons for people in these lodgings, so we
get on nicely.

'Newbridge would appear to have nothing fit to sustain life except what the confectioner provides. All the ladies of the regiment send to Dublin for supplies, but Cyril votes that all nonsense, and has set a pleasing example of buying everything at Newbridge, so I hope it will agree with us.

'We got some skating whilst the frost lasted, which, like everything in Ireland, was very capricious and uncertain. The river here has so rapid a current that it was hard to get it to freeze; but the canal behaved better, though it was unsafe except just in the middle, and we had to use long planks as bridges and then to skate "ahead." There was not much room for figures. We all enjoyed it as best we could, though for skating I must say it was as bad as it could be. Captain Beaumont was very kind,—he had a long ladder and two or three men always ready in case of emergency, and George Harris took my other hand. Of course Cyril had one, and we three "went the pace."

'Our neighbours are said to be hospitable. Many came and looked at us on the ice, but did not join. I think they could not; though I am told it was on account of religious scruples. We drove ten miles last night to a large house called by a very Irish name, where the Honourable Mrs Something Somebody entertained us with very weak tea, and not even bread and butter. I suppose Honourables in this country do not require sustentation, but I was very hungry after our drive, and began wearily to ask Cyril whether we were to have supper. He put up his eyeglass at me, but said nothing. Captain Beaumont went to the servants, I fancy, and found out that there was nothing to hope for beyond what we had had, namely, a little tea and a very little music, and so we drove home,—Cyril, Captain Beaumont, George Harris and I to our rooms, where we got up a heavy tea. It was only twelve o'clock, and oh dear! it was very welcome. I conclude that lady thought that the honour and glory of her presence was enough for us; but, as Cyril says, "it was not."

'There were several persons from the village near and several aristocratic girls, cold and stupid, who thought their fine names would do instead of exertion, for their music was very bad, ill practised, and carelessly performed.

'Cyril says all the ladies about tell him "dinners are gone out of fashion," so I suppose we are to look for tea, like Mrs the Honourable's.'

The next letter said—

'We have been to a ball! An old Captain Dandybrook has an ancient daugther and a new house to warm for her, so he got out some of us to aid and abet.

'I suppose some new invention of the evening prompted this ancient lady to dread that I might feel hungry, for her first bit of information was—

' "We never give dinners at Old-bridgeville,—they are quite out of fashion."

' " Is tea out of fashion, too ? " I asked in the most innocent of tones, and if Cyril had not put up his glass at me I should have had some fun.

' Wherever we go the first information is—" We dine at two o'clock." I fancy they think the English are always on the look-out for dinners, so act on the defensive. I am sure I do not want to trouble the poor people at all, and I know they ask me because of Cyril and Captain Beaumont and George Harris,—it is a great thing to get three beaux and only one lady; most men have two, and some are deluded enough to take three, and as the enemy's camp about here is composed of old maids, I understand all about it, you see.

' George Harris says he was here in his youth, and now dances with the tender

creatures who nurtured him in infancy.
Well, commend me to Oldbridgeville for
ladies between seven and twenty and
seven and fifty, who all will dance.

'I want you to bring over Fairy and
Posy, and let me have them at my ball, for
I am going to give a very pretty one, and
have a good supper too!

'Captain Beaumont is terribly out of
spirits,—some domestic affairs worry him, I
fancy; but what worries him more is the
dead-set the Newbridge chaperones have
made at him. George Harris has written a
play about it, and when we get to England
he says he intends to bring it out. Boast-
ing of what they used to do "before the
famine" is the principal amusement of
families here. I suppose they and the
members are all so old that a period of
twenty years makes no difference. George
Harris is always making pretended mistakes,
and relating what they said as if "before
the flood!" They seem rather to like it,

and drink up any sort of flattery. We know a good many families now in the neighbourhood, but never see more than two or three at a time, for the principal ones are usually having a " coolness," and will not meet each other. There is one very charming woman who comes to see us sometimes, who is condemned by them all, and I like her because she does not "have a coolness" with them, but I believe she is independent, having a *heart full* of children and occupations. She is called Effie Wynne, and her husband is absent somewhere; but she is so fond of him. It has been difficult for me to get to see her, but I managed it.

'I suppose Posy and Fairy had better not come. Did you ever hear that to be an officer's wife is to be wicked?

'Yesterday I heard a voice say to our servant, "Is Major Brembridge at home?"

'"No, Madame. Mrs Brembridge is."

'The door opened, and a lady in black

entered, with an air of scorn and a face of disgust.

' " I am the clergyman's wife," she said, " we do not generally call upon officers and their wives, for we think they are such wicked people."

'I do not remember what I said. I hope nothing wicked! I suppose some spirit of ladyism came to the rescue, but I was very glad when Mrs L'Estranger went away. I told Cyril when he came in; he put up his glass at me and looked into my face, then put his dear arms round me, and gave me a kiss. If I were wicked, Cyril would have a better chance of making me good than the poor virtuous lady in black!'

' Are Posy and Fairy to go to Ireland?' Bessie asked, after Mr Morton Langdale had made many jests about the wickedness of his sister-in-law, of whom he was very fond.

'No,' he said; 'Cyril may not remain

at Newbridge any time, but be ordered to
Belfast or back to Dublin, and I do not
care to take my pretty young maidens to
be contrasted with the ladies who form the
present entourage of my wife's sister.'

Rudolf wrote a good deal of the same
kind to Bessie, and told her Newbridge
news, such as it was.

' The ladies are all jealous about a new
proprietor, who is also an Honourable, and
about as generous as the lady to whose
house you have no doubt heard we went.
He gives musical tea-parties, and the whole
thing is too absurd! these creatures actually live so separately from their neighbours, that they believe their music is
worth hearing; whereas to us, who have
heard better, it is worse than mediocre.
The new proprietor has eyes only for one
lady, who has refused him twice, and I
leave you to think what such a set say of
her. She has the kindest of hearts, but it
is not safe from calumny. "We do not

know her" is usually said by these tender ones, when they have said their say.

'Bessie, I would rather hide you, my darling, in the bulrushes or anywhere, than bring you in contact with such people as we have here. Keep quiet, dearest,—our secret is very sweet and sacred. I consider this a detestable neighbourhood. I hope all Ireland is not as full of gossip and scandal. Here to do a kind act is to lay oneself open to positive slander. Think of the vulgarity, —I have had about forty valentines, and George Harris goes about declaring he has had fourteen offers of marriage. He is as sick of Ireland as I am, and not at all likely to give in to the allurements of New-bridge; he says he shall sell out, to avoid Lady Danger, if they keep us longer in this country.

'Old days, Bessie, and lovers' tales are gone; stiffness, want of candour, and a general wish to subdue all neighbourly in-

stinct, is unfortunately the character of the
upper class in Ireland.

'Of the lower I speak as I always did,
—they are faithful and true, but have bad
rulers and evil drivers. "It is all a hopeless
case," as Mrs Brembridge says. I am only
so glad you are not here, longing though
I am for us to be near each other. All
these weeks have gone and no letter from
Bob, no news of my father, and, what is
becoming very terrible, no arrangement of
money matters.'

Bessie turned to her duties with a sigh,
Fairy and Posy had to sing, and to play,
and to recite, and to translate, and all the
time they did so Bessie gave them full
attention; but a moment came when the
hour was over and she was free.

'I cannot walk with you to-day,' she
said, and Fairy and Posy, nothing loth,
went out with the ponies, that were always ready for such days, and a trusty

old serving man rode with them.

Bessie for once left all her books and papers on her table, and threw herself upon the sofa, to think over all sorts of events and circumstances.

'Rudolf is sick of prejudice,' she said, 'and I have no wish to go to Ireland, except to make him happier. Oh, money, money! if we had only money I could be with him, and all the prejudices of twenty Irelands should not keep me from him.'

It was a fine bright afternoon, and Mrs Morton Langdale had gone with the carriage to pay some distant visits, Bessie lay as aforesaid, thinking, on the sofa, and the two young ladies were riding, not in best hats and habits, as when they rode their horses with papa, but in grey winsey habits and weather-beaten head-gear, which was kept for such expeditions as the present.

How it all happened nobody seemed to know. Both girls were able to ride anything; but Posy, whose pony was quiet

and manageable, got thrown, and her little
ankle was injured.

A large broad man was riding slowly
along the road, talking to a country cattle-
driver. He dismounted, and gave his horse
to the cattle-driver, saying,

' Go quietly on. I shall overtake you
at Dudley burn.'

The broad man then took Posy in his
arms, and, without a word, followed Fairy,
who was yet on her pony, and the old
groom, who led Posy's little delinquent
steed.

Fairy left hers at the door, and ran up
the stairs with her swift and silent tread to
the room where Bessie was—asleep now,
after her fit of thinking.

Both the girls felt the broad man was a
gentleman.

He, with Posy poised in his great arms,
saw the lady, the school-room, the papers
and letters on the table, in one instant.
A letter of Rudolf's lay open—an envelope

addressed to Rudolf. Both these facts showed him that the lady could be no stranger. She opened her eyes, and knew who he must be. Rising from the sofa, she said,

'I am very much obliged to you.' And Posy was gently laid in her place.

'Fairy, call Nurse; I hope there is not much the matter,' Bessie said.

'I don't believe there is anything the matter,' said Posy, whose pretty face was stained with tears, which had come more of vexation than of pain.

Nurse took off her boot and stocking, for she had been with the girls since their babyhood, and saw the broad form of Mc-Laughlan, and did not feel afraid of him.

'You shall rest for to-day,' said Nurse; 'to-morrow you will be well.'

'Let me carry her up-stairs,' said Mc-Laughlan with the cool instinct which was his second nature.

He did so, and then returned to Bessie and said,

'Can you put away your papers and show me the road to Dudley burn? You have not been out to-day?'

'No. I will come. Of course you are Mr McLaughlan?' she added in a low voice.

He nodded, and she saw he did not wish to say more.

She put away her papers and letters, then called to Fairy and said,

'Fairy, I am going to show the gentleman the turn to Dudley burn.'

'Do,' answered Fairy; 'he might take the wrong one at the cross roads.'

So Bessie and McLaughlan left the house together.

Time was short;—he began at once.

'I think you are the wife, or to be the wife, of Robert Beaumont or his brother? Where is Robert now?'

Bessie told him how it seemed impossible to find the father, and of Robert's fruitless search, and how the lawyer had insisted on his leaving Canada, and of the wreck of the 'Iscambria,' then of Rudolf's continued stay in Ireland.

'And you?' he said.

'I remain here,' Bessie replied; 'tell me how you came to Morton Langdale.'

'By reason of my fallen fortunes, too; I am doing a trade as a butcher, in fact, Mrs Beaumont.'

Bessie blushed brilliantly, but did not make any further sign.

'I do not quite understand,' she said.

'I lent money,' said McLaughlan, 'to a scoundrel, and I have to do the best I can; but it is very inconvenient to me. Give me your brother in—give me, in fact, Rudolf Beaumont's address.'

Bessie gave it; he entered 'Newbridge, Ireland,' in his pocket-book.

'Which of the Beaumonts do you wish

to see first?' asked McLaughlan in his own honest way.

'Rudolf,' said Bessie, equally honest, and trusting him.

'If Rudolf came to London under peculiar circumstances would you join him?'

'I would,' said Bessie.

'Or Robert?'

'I could not.'

'Yet Robert—' He was going to say something about the bit of pink flower, but stopped, and considered that perhaps she did not know.

'I am married to Rudolf,' said dear honest Bessie, seeing the situation had become oppressive, 'but we have to keep it secret, for he gets no money but his pay, and I can earn a hundred a year, but people would not like a married governess, —so Rudolf says.'

'And where is Robert?'

'Poor Bob! at Copenhagen, I believe.

And you, Mr McLaughlan, went to New York?'

'Yes; I went in the " City of Washington," and came back. It was rather hard to find I had been deceived again.'

' How so ? '

'I had lent some money. I need not tell you about my affairs. If I get Rudolf to London will you join him ? '

'I will, gladly. If I am not—' she continued.

' What ? '

' An encumbrance to him.'

' God bless you. You will not be that! You will have to give up society, and that sort of thing.'

' Will Rudolf be happy ? '

' I mean him to be so.'

' Mr McLaughlan, I trust you.'

' Thank you. Now go back, Mrs Beaumont,—it is far enough for you to walk; you may give notice if you like. At any rate I, McLaughlan, undertake to have

Rudolf in a home for you within two months.'

'In London?'

'Yes; why?'

'Only he does not care for Ireland.'

'Can you keep this meeting secret?'

'I can if you wish it.'

'It will be better for all parties.'

'Then it shall be so.   Good-bye, Mr McLaughlan.'

He raised his hat to her and passed quickly out of sight.

Bessie returned in time to see Mrs Morton Langdale drive up to the door. She told at once of Posy's trifling accident, and that she had been to show the stranger the road to Dudley burn.

'He was such a nice strong man, mamma,' said Fairy.

'Posy is not a very great weight,' said the mother, light of heart, to find there was no further harm done.

So McLaughlan's visit left no trace

with Posy and Fairy or their mother, who took the whole matter as it looked to them, whereas Bessie had a new and bounding sympathy with every hour that passed; 'it will soon be over,' was the refrain.   The time of separation was running out so fast, and the sweet secret seemed to be doubly sweet since she had confided it to Mr McLaughlan.

'He knows at any rate that I am Rudolf's wife, and I can trust him;' and day followed day, and Bessie grew very sanguine, and wondered where the home would be which McLaughlan had promised her in two months' time.

She trusted so implicitly, this friend McLaughlan, that she told Mrs Morton Langdale that in two months she was to go home.

Vague was the idea in her mind; but home is a word which has tender associations, and Mrs Morton Langdale asked no questions. Posy and Fairy asked, ' Are you going to your mother?' And Bessie said, 'I hardly know how it will all be yet, only, Posy, I am going home, so let us get these books all finished by the time I have to go.'

CHAPTER III.

THE SHOP IN LONDON.

IT comes easily to be understood that Rudolf, sick of Ireland and of separation from Bessie, should agree to any sort of proposal on the part of McLaughlan, whose strong will never seemed to find obstacles with the honest Rudolf, Robert, and Bessie.

It may appear that a very great struggle must have taken place with Rudolf and Bessie; but it was not so. It was all to gain, and nothing to lose for both of them; tried, separated, and weary as both were of poverty and the effort to keep things up, Rudolf especially knew

the bitterness, for his expensive regiment
and Irish quarters drained his pay, and
Robert must have something sent to keep
life going, little as he seemed to require.

McLaughlan had arranged everything :
had furnished a sitting-room and a chamber with elegance for Bessie, had talked
over all matters with Rudolf, who became,
under his direction, Mr Joshua Ribbs, and
the united Rudolf and Bessie took possession of their home with a feeling of thankfulness, that had something like adoration
for McLaughlan combined.   Rudolf had
dreaded that the want of experience would
betray him.

'So it would,' said McLaughlan, 'in an
inferior establishment. Recollect, you have
to make use of the deportment of a swell,
wear a diamond ring if you please. You
are master of the situation,—nothing will
be attributed to you, but to your foreman,
whom you can blame *ad libitum*.

Master of the situation Rudolf appeared

to be; affairs went on smoothly, he could
manage the accounts easily, the foreman
supposing him to be a veritable Joshua
Ribbs, and himself an honest man, with a
wife and family to provide for, John Davis
did his duty honestly, and as one good
honest life always does good, the boys
believed in him, and things which Rudolf
had dreaded went wonderfully smoothly.

'I often wonder,' Bessie said, 'that no
one recognizes you, Rudolf!'

'My dear,' he replied, 'people never
think of me. Having left the army, I am
dis-remembered, as they say in Ireland.
The fellows of my own regiment never
think of me, since I do not go to see them.
Major Brembridge or even George Harris
might step into our sawdust-covered establishment, and seeing an individual in a
blue apron, and a steel dangling by his
side, would deliver the order and never
notice the wearer. Bessie, we have chosen
the safest plan,—we are not likely to be

recognized, and when the time comes for you to return to society, no recollection of Mr Joshua Ribbs will occur.'

'But we cannot cheat society,' said honest Bessie.

'At present I see but little chance of our returning to it; do you mind it, Bessie?'

'I would rather be *my* butcher's wife,' she said, lovingly pressing his arm.

'For the present, my darling, we have chosen, as I said, a safe plan,—our obscurity will keep us quite out of the field of view of former acquaintances, and should the right time occur, we can return to our proper sphere, and forget Mr Joshua Ribbs.'

'I shall never forget him,' Bessie said, 'and for myself, you know it is such rest. I did not think I could have been so happy in idleness.'

'Some day,' Rudolf said, 'if we have children, it will be important to consider the world, which does not tolerate the earning of one's bread either in man or woman, except in one routine sort of manner. We can wait, my Bessie; but do not fret about going out again. One hundred a year is the most you could make; and what is a man who would let his wife work?'

'And you think,' said Bessie, 'if you had children it would go against them?'

'Yes, Bessie, if things ever come that I can resume my own position.'

'I understand. I am not to share our work,' said Bessie, 'now I am acknowledged to be your wife.'

'Does society ever forgive a woman who earns her bread?'

'I understand, Rudolf.'

'I am not ungrateful, darling; but take your rest. Here you are in peaceful obscurity, and might be in another hemisphere, for anything your former friends may tell. Leave it to me now, my poor hard-worked, ill-used treasure,—I meant to be so proud of you!'

'Ill usage agrees with me,' said Bessie cheerfully; and like a wise woman, she smiled and left it all to her husband. The fact was, he would not part with her again, and made excuses to himself for keeping her, and who can blame him? He had been satisfied, and felt very proud to win the affections of Bessie, though he knew she was at the time in the position of governess to Ella Storton; but those were happy days of ignorance, when society and the world were all before him, and doubt and dread as yet unborn. He knew that Bessie was by birth of equal rank with himself, but having learned the world, he knew that, had she daughters, it would not be reflected upon them that their mother was a noble woman, who had earned her bread and kept herself entirely independent by her own exertions, but rather that 'she was a governess, so has cast a stigma on her children.'

Rudolf wondered at himself, too, as much as he wondered at the change of opinion concerning Bessie. It was a strange power which McLaughlan held over him; a power which raised him in his own estimation, and made a noble something within him rise to the occasion, and fit him to work, to do, and to suffer, for those he loved.

Helga the ubiquitous had soon discovered all the facts; of course she had been sent for, and had helped to establish Bessie in her new home, and she soon acknowledged the hand that had provided for her treasure's wants.

'My lamb! these things are all new; this chamber has been furnished for yourself by one who cares for your likes and dislikes.'

'I thought—I hoped,' said Bessie, 'we took it just as it stood.'

'No, indeed, my lamb! that would

have been smoky and dirty. The paper is fresh, the chintz is new, everything is new; it has been nicely done, and by one who has studied a woman's taste. He is a gentleman, whoever he may be!' Helga added, for she knew there was to some extent a mystery.

'He is a gentleman,' Bessie replied; and then they looked over the sitting-room, which was prepared so carefully, and arranged Bessie's books and various belongings.

A short time followed of success, for Rudolf accepted his new character gravely, and took up his part with discretion and zeal.

McLaughlan had again disappeared, but he had given John Davis information which concerned cattle dealing, and both Rudolf and Bessie believed that McLaughlan himself was the principal and guide in all the transactions. The Danish Banking Company's office was again open, and

through it came the news of M. Brinkmann's death at the Danish island of Saint
Thomas.

'Your mother had better come here,'
said Rudolf.

'Can we make her happy?' asked
Bessie.

'Oh, Bessie! happy? with you?'

And in a few weeks Madame Brinkmann came, and was called Mrs Rockingham, because it was better to carry out the
play of Mr Joshua Ribbs with the cha-
racters complete.

The Danish mother had suffered everything; rash and reckless speculations from
the first had created discord—and but that
she trusted Helga, her heart would have
been torn about her child.

Madame Brinkmann could never leave
her husband: he was one of those men
who cannot stand alone,—he wanted her
continually, and she kept by him to the
last. Failure and uncertainty, the loss of

other little ones, were all forgotten when she met and embraced Bessie.

The terrible hurricane which swept Saint Thomas washed away the Brinkmann's villa; he was then ill, and died of exposure and the shock. Madame became helpless by rheumatism, but had to suffer yet more before her rest could come. The steamer, 'Falkner,' foundered at sea; she was one who was saved, but the open-boat navigation cramped and wore her out. She arrived in London, but a cripple, and so remained.

Helga stayed to see her friend as happily established as possible, and then returned to Denmark. She said, ' You have your husband and your mother now, my lamb. I yearn for Denmark, and must stay there for the rest of my life. I shall miss my lamb.'

' Stay with us, Helga,' Rudolf said.

' No; you have my lamb,—she is quite safe. I ought to go to Nikel, and Anna

Magnusen and other friends are married, and will want to confer with a woman of experience!' So Helga, gay and useful, having seen Bessie settled in London, left, to resume her Danish character.

Mrs Rockingham, as she came to be known in the very little circle which closed in Bessie and her husband, soon became aware of all the particulars they could give concerning the Scandinavian Ring, and declared that she gave in to the superstition concerning it, and fully believed that the reappearance of it would be the signal for the revival of the fallen fortunes of the Beaumont family.

A great many books are published about Northern people, Vikings, and such heroes, and Hans Anderson has made us familiar with life in Jutland. We can acknowledge the similarity of human nature in Denmark and in England, and need not read more of Helga's letters, which told Bessie about Anna's garden and her roses and coming baby, but added that she could make out nothing of the dear old Mr Beaumont. Then she ran on about a female artist, who, from her room in Thorwaldsen Street, sent forth such pictures as quite astonished the world, and raised the fame of Denmark in the world of art.

'I hope,' the letter said, 'she is Danish, but at any rate we claim her now. She is going to send a picture to Paris when the Exposition opens, and our new academy here is beautified with several. I want very much to see her, but no one has the *entrée* to her studio ; they say she refused to see even the English Prince. She has written also something which pleases the powers that be at Copenhagen about our Danish poets Ewald, Wessel, and Begessen, and declares that Danish writers are very natural and picturesque.'

Thus Helga was a frequent correspondent; so it was natural that Bessie should write to her when the illucid letter, signed

'Bob,' arrived about the child, and the reply was awaited with much impatience.

No letter came in reply. It happened that Helga was absent, and the delay was one which surprised Rudolf and Bessie very much, and Mrs Rockingham was quite distressed on finding how much her daughter suffered from this suspense.

'I think, my dear, you expect the child to bring you the ring?'

'What if it should?' said Bessie, 'it would be so delightful to know where it is!'

Cattle and trade occupied Rudolf, who got a mysterious epistle from McLaughlan, who was gone now to Monte Video, on a monster cattle speculation, and intended to join a settlement which would start from Rosario on a certain day.

McLaughlan had become a sort of wandering deity in Bessie's eyes.

'I am sorry he is gone so far,' she said, 'but I know that he will be instrumental in

restoring our fortunes, so he is sure to return.'

'How do you know?'

'I cannot tell,' said Bessie, 'but I do
know it. I believe in Mr McLaughlan,
as I did that day on which he carried Posy
up-stairs at Morton Langdale.'

'And called you Mrs Beaumont?'

'Yes, it was very clever of him to do
so. How could he tell? Rudolf, could he
have been present at our quiet marriage
that morning in London?'

'I think not; but never mind how he
found you,—he did it cleverly and well.'

'Do you think,' said Bessie, with the
geranium glowing in her cheeks, 'that he
was in the direction of Morton Langdale
to look for me?'

'I do not know, Bessie, but it looks
very like it.'

Further conversation was prevented by
a call from the shop door.

'Wanted, sir, if you please.'

Rudolf found a porter from the railway awaiting him.

'I have a strange little freight here, sir.'

'What is it? alive or dead?' for Mr Joshua Ribbs expected it to be some precious carcase, or animal soon to become so.

'Better than that, I fancy, sir,' said the porter, who went to a cab which was standing at the door and brought forth a lovely little girl half asleep, who blinked as her eyes encountered the gas in the light shop.

'Is she alone?' asked Mr Ribbs.

'Quite, sir, all the way from Hull. There is a ticket sewed to her jacket with your address.'

Rudolf opened a large blue cloak which enfolded the child, and read on a card fastened to her dress—

To the care of Mr Joshua Ribbs,

40, Upper Dane Street,

London.

Rudolf called the porter aside, but he could only tell how the guard had put the child into his charge, and told him to see her safely to that address.

'She's a good little creature, sir, as good as gold,' said the man, taking the gratuity from Rudolf as he spoke.

'Is there any luggage?'

'Nothing: there is only herself; I expect you will get particulars to-morrow,' said the porter, who, having delivered his goods, felt himself free to depart.

The child was standing on a bench where she had been set from the arms of the man when he pointed out the address to Rudolf. Only John Davis was present, who said,—

'What a little beauty she is, sir!'

'Yes, my little Danish friend must be sleepy.'

'No, I am not,' said the child in English.

'Are you hungry, then?'

'Oh no, Monsieur; they tried to feed me all the way since I left the ship till I got here.'

'Who did?'

'All the people.'

Rudolf took her in his arms to carry her to Bessie.

'I can walk,' she said, 'if you take off this cloak.'

Rudolf could not manage the fastenings. John Davis stepped forward with—

'Excuse me, sir, allow me;' and he, accustomed to strings and hooks, set the little one free; she put out her pretty face and kissed him, saying—

'Thank you, sir; good night.'

Then Rudolf led her through the baize door to Bessie and her mother.

'The child is safe at any rate, Bessie; here she is,' he said.

And Bessie looked at her.

'She does not belong to Robert, but

her eyes are in some way familiar to me,' was Bessie's verdict to herself.

'You little darling!' was what she said aloud. 'What is your name?'

'Senza.'

'Senza! is that your name?'

'Yes, Senza Beaumont.'

Rudolf started.

'What shall we do—Bessie? that name will never do,—we shall be in danger.'

'She will forget it; we can call her Rockingham,' said Bessie, and a sad feeling fell on them both, of wonder who this child could be. She had dark eyes, but they were very soft and mild, and dark hair, long and silky, but with a gentle yielding manner. Looking a little pale after her journey, Senza, with her strange name and weird appearance, was a sensational episode in the establishment in Upper Dane Street.

'Who put you into the train at Hull,

and fastened the address upon your jacket?' Rudolf asked her.

'Captain Wilson,' said the child.   But she knew no more, not even the name of the steamer, and Mrs Rockingham said they ought not to excite her with questions to-night, so Bessie and the neat maid-servant got a little resting-place for her ready, and placed her in it.

'I wish I knew where the child comes from,' Rudolf said to Mrs Rockingham.

'Perhaps you will some day.   Bessie is satisfied.'

'If I were sure of that,' he said, 'I should be; but I do not like her to take charge of—anybody's child,' he added after a pause.

'I should think your brother could not have sent *anybody's* child, for is he not very fond of Bessie?'

'That is true,' said Rudolf, comforted; 'poor Bob!'

'Poor Bob!' echoed Bessie coming into

the room, 'he has sent us something he thought worth caring for, Rudolf; come and see the pretty nest we have made for her.'

Rudolf went. Some little time elapsed. They came back and told Mrs Rockingham the little creature had fallen asleep the moment her head touched the pillow.

'She is a dear little thing, Rudolf; think of her face, her eyes, her hair. She is a little bigger now, but I believe she is the original of Madame Jerickan's picture child whom the Danish sailor saved from the shipwreck.'

'She may be, my romantic Bessie.'

'How I lingered before that picture last October, and in one of Helga's old letters she told me about a lady who was going to send a picture to the Paris Exhibition, and now having seen the child in the picture, I feel I have the same in reality.'

'You so generally judge truly, my

wife, that I can say nothing; however, let
me go and dismiss Davis; it is getting late,
and is time to close for the night,' and
the baize door only separated husband and
wife, and Bessie's womanly heart sang an
evensong of thanksgiving over the coming
of this pretty little stranger, who was to be
called for the present ' Senza Rockingham.'
She knew it would not do to try to alter
the familiar name, or the child might re-
bel, and bring out the name of Beaumont,
which she had said was hers, and for many
reasons that was one it were better not to
parade at present in the house or establishment of Mr Joshua Ribbs.

CHAPTER IV.

ROSARIO.

THE very next morning came to Bessie a letter from Helga, which said—

'My lamb must not think I have been unmindful of her. We had a very sad outbreak of small-pox, and Anna Magnusen sent for me to take her little one far away into the country farm, where we stayed quietly for some weeks, and no letters or newspapers were sent to us. It did not occur to me that you were likely to write, or I should have had arrangements made for your letters to be brought to me. I hope by this time you have heard of your brother-in-law; he had the complaint badly,

I have since heard, but do not know more
than that he recovered, which will comfort
you, though probably you have seen him.'
Then followed news of Danish folk dear to
Helga, though unknown to us.

'So Robert had that terrible scourge
small-pox?' said Rudolf; 'no wonder he
thought it was " all up" with him!'

'Poor Robert! I wonder who nursed
him?' said Bessie.

'I hope some experienced hand; most
likely he would enter a hospital, and so
get good care,' Rudolf replied.

'If he did that,' said Mrs Rockingham,
'he would have the best of everything, for
the Danish hospitals are beyond all others.'

'Poor Bob!' said Bessie, tenderly; 'I
see it is for our sake he did not write.
How well he managed to get the dear
little child conveyed to us.'

'Yes; how is she? did she sleep well?'

'So well, Rudolf, that I told Jane to
let her have her sleep well out; I expect

she finds her bed comfortable after being rocked in the cradle of the deep.'

'For which you envy her?'

'I should like it, if you and I *could* go and look for Robert.'

'I will write to the Holy Cross Hospital to-day, if Robert were at Copenhagen.'

'Helga says Altona.'

'You did not tell me that. Bessie, we must wait,—you can wait?'

'Wait? yes, I can wait now, Rudolf. I will go and look for my Posy,—she will be glad to get some breakfast.'

Fresh from her bath sat the Posy, eating a cup of bread and milk, and looking with much composure at Jane, and all the comforts about her.

'I shall call you Posy, for you are like violets and primroses,' said Bessie, as she stooped to kiss the child and led her to the breakfast parlour.

Rudolf held out his hand.

'Good morning, little lady.'

'Good morning; is this the saloon? are you the new captain?'

'I suppose so.   Why?'

'Because Captain Wilson said I should have a new captain to-morrow, and this is to-morrow.'

And so luckily another small difficulty arranged itself, namely, what she was to call Rudolf; from that time she always, and only, called him 'Captain.'

The child became an interest and amusement to every one.   Jane was attentive and kind,—Bessie very wisely let her be so; it was better for the servant to attend to her; and to Mrs Rockingham the little girl was useful : she reached her silks, threaded her needles, held her book, and was a tractable, good little creature.   Those who are conversant with child nature in a healthy state know how little of the past remains with them.   The present absorbs all thought, and in a few days even the ship was quite forgotten, and, with the one blue dress in which she landed, all recollection of Denmark passed away.

It was evident she had been with English people, but with whom? Once or twice she said, 'Is that my papa?' when she saw a tall grey-headed gentleman during her early walk with Bessie in the park, for Bessie and Posy walked from nine to ten every fine day, and sometimes, when tempted by the weather, they would remain out till eleven.

After closing time husband and wife sometimes stepped out together for an hour for exercise and a quiet bit of talk. Rudolf was not unhappy, though he felt the false position in which he had to maintain his wife, but the antidote was so very sweet.

Bessie was beside him, sharing his poverty, hidden with him from all the rancour and annoyance of the world : a man and his wife can face anything together.

Meanwhile McLaughlan, when in New York on the trip with the 'City of Washington,' whither he went as a common sailor, met with a medical man who was bound for Rosario.

A settlement of Englishmen was to be attempted, and, with every prospect of success, they flocked out, long before the public papers gave notice that the Argentine Republic was more than a name.

They were to be men of good family, and each capable of furnishing funds for preliminary expenses, and a doctor and clergyman were to go with them.

McLaughlan, whose judgment was to be relied upon, was requested by some of the prudent ones to go at once and arrange with her Majesty's Chargé d'Affaires at Buenos Ayres, and settle a sort of prospectus, upon which heads of families might work with a degree of confidence, and know what they were likely to expect from the farms, and what price would be put

upon them beforehand, a certain gentleman having guaranteed the repayment of
all fees from the profits of the first year,
and more enterprising persons still having given out that gold fields were lying
fallow, waiting only for the soil to be
touched to produce immense profits.

McLaughlan, trusted, and proud of his
embassy, and in sufficient funds with his
cattle dealing and traffic to afford the time,
since his energy and the means he had
acquired of knowing where to get them,
had brought fresh herds into England
after the cattle plague was stayed, proceeded from Liverpool to the South-east
coast of America, and time and tide
went on.

The Argentine Republic is now well
known. The Parana river has been ex-
plored, and new charts have succeeded old
ones. Paraguay and Uruguay, Lopez, and
since his death, Lopez Jordan have filled
the papers with interest, and the wars of

the Blancos and Colorados are as well known as the shipments of Monte Video beef.

McLaughlan went to reconnoitre before all was known, and sent home a serious recommendation to the Emigration Commissioners *not* to permit the undertaking to go on, for it would only end in disappointment.

Good advice is not always taken, nor is foresight acknowledged. They who were eager to go were furious with McLaughlan for proving to them what they did not wish to acknowledge. They called him a 'wet blanket,' and a 'blundering Irishman,' so instead of the effect the few had anticipated, the contrary resulted from his mission to Rosario.

'We only want money,' they said, so they found money; and in spite of McLaughlan's prediction, that the colony would break up very shortly, they determined to found it at any rate; and even

the brisk and busy streets of Liverpool had
an accession of activity, whilst the colonists were shipping themselves and their
supplies.

Very few greeted McLaughlan with
thanks for his information. He had done
his duty; sought out facts which his perfect command of Spanish enabled him to
do, and one of his bits of advice was, to
study that language before they set out;
but they laughed him to scorn. 'We shall
all be English,' they said, so McLaughlan
shrugged his shoulders.

'You can do nothing against the tide
of ignorance but educate it,' he said
quietly; 'and if you will not take experience, you must purchase it.'

CHAPTER V.

OLD FRIENDS.

M^cLAUGHLAN gave his uncle, the Baron, no tidings of his whereabouts; indeed he gave him up, and Ireland on his account; he had found him out, in fact, and knowing him to be a hypocrite, and neither in character nor substance what he professed to be, he washed his hands of the connection, and stood alone.

As to the interference of his uncle, Mr Brett, or the defalcation of Wilson, he took the whole as a bad debt, and filed it.

With this mercantile settlement of his Daneton affairs, he threw all the energy of his nature into a determination to restore the Beaumonts to their rights. For Robert Beaumont he had the romantic attachment which human nature does permit to exist sometimes between two men.

'I would have given my soul for him,' he said.

When he could not find Robert, who had been induced to go to Denmark in search of family information, McLaughlan turned to Rudolf and watched Bessie with much interest after he had been the means of placing them in Number 40 Establishment.

'Will she be able to stand it?' is the question he asked himself, 'or shall I find her worn and pale and discontented, like most women are, with her lot?'

This he said to himself as he drove by the night train from Liverpool to London.

'Will she stand to her part as Mrs Joshua Ribbs? that is the question!' he repeated as the steam and smoke and noise went on. 'If she can hold on a little longer, I feel and know something will turn up.'

Soon after ten o'clock next morning McLaughlan, looking very like the roughest of common sailors, stepped into the saw-dust arena in which Rudolf was playing his part.

Recognition was instantaneous, but not even John Davis could have detected that it was so.

Rudolf went on talking to an old gentleman who was giving orders.

John Davis spoke to McLaughlan.

'Can I do anything for you, sir?'

'I have a parcel from Liverpool, sir, for the lady—for Mrs Ribbs.'

John Davis made the fact known to Mr Joshua.

Rudolf came forward. The blue eyes were so blue, that McLaughlan's glistened in sympathy.

The baize door hid them both from view, and John Davis did not know that

Rudolf, blue apron, steel, and all, threw himself upon McLaughlan's shoulder.

'My dear, dear old fellow!' he said.

'Well, how are you getting on?' was the reply.

'Where is—?'

'Bessie.'

'Yes, Mrs—'

'Out with the child.'

'Where?'

Rudolf told,—the park.

'May I go and meet her?'

'If you like.'

'Would she be ashamed to walk with a sailor?'

'She would not be ashamed to walk with you.'

Bessie came in, driven back by a shower, to endorse the sentiment.

'Oh, I am so glad to see you,' she said.

McLaughlan took her pretty gloved hand and raised it, for amongst the bush of beard and moustaches he is supposed to have had lips.

He looked at the child, a pretty little walking child.

'Is it not a very fine one?' he said, with a pleasant wonder in his eyes.

Bessie's geraniums rushed into bloom.

'She is a little waif from Denmark,' Rudolf said.

McLaughlan stared at all three.

'What is your name, Miss?' he asked of the little lady in a white frock with pink ribbons.

'Senza Speranza Beaumont, sir.'

'The tiny face looked up to his with positive dignity, and she actually put emphasis on the sir,' said Rudolf, telling the circumstance later to Mrs Rockingham; 'we never had her full name before; "Senza Speranza!" How plainly the atom can speak!'

'It surprises me above all,' said Mrs

Rockingham, 'that her tongue is English, and of so pure an accent; had she lived with common people we should have had a different intonation. I think your brother Robert must have married, Rudolf, and hearing from this Mr McLaughlan, who is his friend, that you and Bessie are here, he sent the baby beauty to be taken care of here.'

'Senza Speranza,' Rudolf repeated; 'it is, I trust, not a hopeless care either. I am not afraid of anything since we have seen McLaughlan again.'

'He is one of your superstitions.'

'One of my superstitions, yes. I never meet him without being the better for it.'

'His influence is like a prayer,' said Bessie, placing her lovely head on Rudolf's shoulder.

'My dear!' said Mrs Rockingham.

'I know what Bessie means,—it is a sort of thing that keeps one up.'

'I understand you now,' the mother said.

'And,' continued Rudolf, 'that man has power; he is something to lean against, like a great rock.'

'Yet he has not been prosperous in the world!' said Mrs Rockingham.

'Well, no; but my simile holds good still,—he is a rock, and the waves have gone over him, and he has stood the shock, and is as hard and sound as ever.'

'How good little Posy was with him; I half expected her to be afraid of his great beard.'

'Children only look at people's eyes,' said Mrs Rockingham.

'All the rest,' added Rudolf laughing, 'beard and whiskers, and great rough coat, go for nothing.'

'Go to support the eyes,' said Bessie, looking into Rudolf's, who blushed like a boy, and looked at his blue cuffs and apron.

McLaughlan came next day; he said,
' I am so rough, I fear you will hardly like
to have me; but recollect, there is a warrant
out against me for the charge of arson, and
I am very anxious to set some matters
right, so accept me in disguise.'

' You are never in disguise to us,' said
Bessie, who then told him all she knew
about the Posy, who was gone to bed, for
it was evening now, and less inconvenient
for Rudolf to receive a long visit.

' I want to do one thing before I leave
England,' said McLaughlan, ' then I must
go for Robert.'

' What is the one thing?'

' With your permission, seek particulars
of Beaumont Grange.'

' I can give none. It is Robert's, or
should be; but you are aware the deeds
have been stolen; the lawyer is afraid to
stir in the affair, and ruin and desolation
must have attacked the place.'

' Mr McLaughlan,' said Bessie, ' you

must find the Scandinavian Ring for us,
then everything will come right.'

'Why do you say this to *me*, Mrs
Beaumont? surely you do not suspect—'

'My dear sir! what do you mean?'

'I hardly know; but I saw that ring in
the old tulip cabinet, which I afterwards
bought, and it was, unluckily, burnt at my
great fire at Daneton. The ring seems to
have affected me as much as any of you.'

'Well, find it for us all.'

'Why do you say this?'

'Because you can do anything you
will,' said Bessie.

'Mrs Beaumont, you are too good.
You put too high a motive upon all your
friends' actions.'

'Not if they live up to them,' said Rudolf.

'You surprise me very much, Mrs
Beaumont,' McLaughlan observed, after an
hour's talk with her husband; 'I expected
Mr Beaumont would bear the change for

the sake of having you, and a man is so glad to have employment.'

'And did you doubt me?' said Bessie, smiling that peculiar smile of hers; 'did you think I should pine for liberty?'

'I did not think you could stand it.'

'It is only for a time; less painful than a new situation. You forget all that I have gone through. Absence from annoyance is happiness to me, besides being with my husband,' she said proudly.

'And you send me forth on a mission, Mrs Beaumont, to find the Scandinavian Ring?' he said, as he rose to take leave.

'I do.'

'And what is to be my reward?'

'I cannot tell yet, but there will be one, as surely as we see the ring.'

'Do not go yet,' said Rudolf; 'you are not going to hunt for the ring to-night.'

McLaughlan sat down again.

'Do you never go out, Mrs Beaumont?'

'Every morning, unless it rains very hard,' she said.

'I mean never into company, *Society*, as it is called; it is a foolish question, but I like to ask it.'

'I could not go to see Grace Trulybridge,' Bessie said, 'and really I have no other very close friend. Mrs Morton Langdale has as much forgotten me as Major Brembridge has accepted George Harris in Rudolf's place.'

'I suppose so. Do you care?'

'No, I think not.'

'If you ever have a place of your own, you will be very generous.'

'I hope so; but I never shall.'

'Oh yes, you will, when we get the ring.'

Bessie smiled.

'I am glad we have infected you with our superstition,' she said.

'I like a little superstition. I am not

good enough to be religious; but one must have some sort of faith.'

'That is religion,' said Bessie.

'I wish mine were, Mrs Beaumont,' he said with a tender smile. 'Your faith is religion, mine is, I fear, to save the trouble of religion.'

'How so?'

'I mean like the poor people in Ireland cross themselves; that stands for religion; they are very pious.'

'Then the crossing does them good?' said Rudolf.

'I often think so. It is better to have form than nothing.'

'Oh no, Mr McLaughlan,' said Bessie; 'that is a bad superstition.'

'Give me a better.'

'The outward form is only a little token of the great power, without which we could not exist; it is a little acknow-ledgment of the great something which can never be expressed.'

' Then all denominations ought to cross themselves.'

' The cross is the mere symbol of our redemption ; it is well to put oneself under its protection,' Bessie said.

' Under the shadow of the cross ; yes, it is a nice feeling too,' said McLaughlan, musingly.

' Yet your Irishmen abuse it,' said Rudolf. ' Do they not make the sign of the cross on the bullet with which they shoot down their agents in your country ? '

' I fear they do; that is the abuse of superstition.'

' Whereas good superstition is faith, and faith is religion, and religion must be for good,' said Bessie.

' It is easy to be good with you to argue for one. Mrs Beaumont, I have hitherto been amongst those who looked for bad motives instead of good ones; who ill-treated me, took my money, accepted my presents, traded upon my affections, and left me.'

'You have been unfortunate in your friends in Ireland.'

'I fear I have; one whom I trusted with everything, even my honour, took my money under false pretences, and got from me the letter in which he had asked for it.'

'I do not see why,' said Bessie.

'You are too pure to see why. I even did not know at the time how far he had deceived me. Let him go. God forgive him, as I do.'

'That is right; let them all go. You belong to us now, Mr McLaughlan.'

'Do I? and if I find the ring you will not cast me off?'

'We shall never do that, whether you find the ring or not,' said Bessie.

'Thank you.' Then he got up and took their proffered hands, and said, 'Good night.'

CHAPTER VI.

THE GENIUS OF THE RING.

M^cLAUGHLAN, rough in exterior, but softened by contact with Bessie, went to the Beaumonts' family lawyer, and having laid his own case before him, with the trusting camaraderie which teaches one to 'tell all to the lawyer and the doctor,' said how much he had the case of the Beaumonts at heart, and how he believed something would be learned by a visit to Beaumont Grange.

'My good sir, the heir who has turned up so inopportunely would not let you enter.'

'He is abroad, dying, I believe, at

Naples; believe me, I have taken this affair in hand very warmly ; give me leave to run all risks and see what I can make out.'

'What is your plan ?'

'To go in my present character of a common sailor, and enter the place by hook or by crook, and find whether any papers are left there.'

'How about the servants ?'

'If women, I can wheedle them; if men, I can awe them by mere brute force into submission; but I have a feeling that I cannot do this without your instructions.'

'Instructions I cannot give, but I quite agree that something should be done. I induced Robert Beaumont to come from Canada to try and find the father,—he appears to have failed in that. I have heard that he was attacked by small-pox and recovered, since then I have heard nothing of any of the family. Is the second brother in Ireland ?'

'I think the second brother is not of importance; let me proceed to the Grange.'

'When will you go?'

'To-day if you please. You see any day I may be recognized, and then the game is up.'

'I have some duplicate keys, I think, which may be of use;' so the lawyer sought and found some keys, all neatly labelled, and McLaughlan pocketing them, set out for the railway which would take him to Beaumont Grange.

McLaughlan drove up to the deserted mansion on a day that Gustave Doré would have chosen, if he wanted to give a picture of it. Delicate lights, very bright, and a slight mist were everywhere. Each tree stood out against a background of deep, dark blue. Autumn leaves were not yet fallen, but there was a tottering, shimmering promise about them that they would come from their slender stalklets very soon.

Tints gorgeous as those of America

were present, for there were maple and
other trees amongst the oaks and beeches,
and the brushwood and brambles under-
neath had crimson leaves and golden tints,
as well as Bismarck brown. The gates
were all locked, but McLaughlan climbed
over, leaving the hired conveyance on the
road, where he told the man to stay and
feed his horse, and to wait for him for an
hour or two.

The hall door had a knocker and a
bell, and resounding peal and thundering
knock awoke the echoes up within.

There was no trace of humankind; no
servant or care-taker within, or in the
yards without. There was no dog, or
cow, or sign of life, no evidence that life
had been nurtured there for many a day.

The keys of course were for inner rooms
and store places, but a man like Mc-
Laughlan was not to be daunted. He im-
provised a ladder, or what did for one, and
climbing over a portion of a sloping roof,

which covered a scullery or some such place, he entered by a little window, of which, by the fracture of a pane of glass, he could find the fastening.

Some dust and a few dead leaves, that was all he encountered in the empty house.

The keys availed now to open the great rooms. There was less of decay than he had anticipated: people used to build better than they do now, and no damp had penetrated these thick walls.

'What a pity,' said McLaughlan, 'that the poor, sad, ill-spent life which is so fast passing away, should have kept Robert Beaumont out of this nice place, or his father!'

But of the father he knew and cared little, except that Robert's anxiety and frequent journeys to Denmark had wasted his days in disappointment.

McLaughlan had opened some presses, and had sought for deed chests without avail, till his watch and the declining light.

warned him it was time to go. He was about to close up the windows when a door in the wall for the first time attracted him. He opened it,—the room was dark and airless. He had brought a long wax candle and some matches; something prompted him to light it before crossing this chamber to undo the shutters.

In the middle of the room stood a bed, and on it, apparently, a man fast asleep.

It was so close and airless, that McLaughlan yielded to instinct, and unfastened a window before noticing further.

There lay Captain Beaumont.

The poor old man had come home to Beaumont Grange, had let himself in, and died there! Whether ill and no one came near, whether weary and looking for rest, none can tell.

The case may have been very short, or hunger may have been long and severe. Let us hope the former. He may have arrived late at night and expected servants to attend him, and finding them absent, may have lain down for a little time to rest his weary frame just as he was, in all his clothes, with his great coat and a knitted woollen comforter. Thus, whether God called him at once by means of heart complaint or effusion of the brain, or whether it was winter, and the cold took possession of him, he lay there, unattended, and perhaps starvation caused the last long sleep.

There he was, McLaughlan found him. So entirely was the air excluded, that no moths had fretted the garments which shrouded the shrunken form. No rat nor nibbling mouse had touched him.

His gray hair and moustache made him look much like himself, a ring was on his finger, and his watch had stopped at 7.

Possibly he had wound it up on lying down, and it had gone on ticking for twenty-four hours after his heart had ceased to throb!

Perhaps he was very weary; his boots were on his feet, and the woollen comforter betokened that he had journeyed in cold weather, and had perhaps found himself too tired to remove his wrappings, and finding no servants at the Grange, he had meant to sleep as best he could, and so gone supperless to bed.

The shutters were bolted; when he closed the door no doubt he intended to go forth with the morning. But to him the morning never came—on earth. He may have been frozen to death. Terrible thought! His going forth was not to be for many weeks and months. And so he lay. The summer sun beat on those shutters, and dried the air of his mausoleum, the walls were thick, the warmth did not get out; the winter chilled, but did not render the stones damp.

No insects from the outer air had gained admission. No rats, for surely these had fulfilled the prophecy and had deserted the house of the fallen fortunes.

The white hair and the shrunken features were not ghastly to look at, only sad : poor Captain Beaumont !

McLaughlan closed the door and locked it. Then he walked quickly to the hired conveyance, and reached London by a late train.

He was at the door of No. 40, Upper Dane Street, when Rudolf came to play his first part of Mr Joshua Ribbs the next morning.

The two men stood quietly together behind the partition, where Rudolf used to arrange his account-books.

'Your better way is to remain here,' said McLaughlan ; 'let me arrange with your lawyer and do everything, as if you were absent, like Robert.'

'Yes, I see it is. I have no power in any way, and it is better for Bessie, for every one, for you to do all.'

So McLaughlan went to the lawyer,

and then, empowered by him to act for Robert as far as possible, went back.

McLaughlan took it upon himself to call an inquest, and to watch the frail remains, and guard them from the air, till such ceremonies should be over; and a coffin was prepared to receive the unburied dead, and the funeral rites were solemnized as speedily as the formalities would admit.

He was not placed in the family vault, but in the Beaumont Churchyard, as McLaughlan thought, when the sons could be asked the question, they might wish that Captain Beaumont should be taken to the Daneton Cemetery, and be placed beside his Truda.

All such arrangements then being prepared, on the evening after the inquest, having advertised for Captain Beaumont's sons, according to his agreement with the family lawyer, who wanted to have information crop up from all possible quarters concerning the affairs, and having had such magisterial and other advice as circumstances required, McLaughlan himself approached the body, in order to remove the watch and chain, and such things as should not be buried with him.

Then he touched the poor dead hand, and on the third finger was—The Scandinavian Ring!

'And is it thus,' said McLaughlan aloud, 'that I find the ring, of which they have all talked to me, from Robert, who told me of his mother's mentioning to him that I had touched it (and I once fancied he half suspected I had taken it from her, and, only that it was beneath me, I half felt angry, and inclined to lose my temper)? Bessie has spoken of it since! It is the Beaumont mystery. I will take the ring to her, or go with it for Robert, and so restore the fortunes of the family.'

After the quiet funeral Bessie was told the circumstances concerning the finding of the ring. She shed some angel tears over the dear old father, and his lonely death, which took place too long ago to give much pain, and then she said,

'You are our good genius! I am so glad it was you who found the ring.'

'Shall I take it with me, Mrs Beaumont, and bring back Robert?'

'Oh, do, Mr McLaughlan, and tell him how pretty Posy is, and how good and happy.'

'I will. May I see her to-day?'

Posy was called, and came laden with dolls.

McLaughlan caught her in his arms.

'Oh!' exclaimed Bessie.

'What now? I shall not hurt her.'

'I like it, Bessie,' said the baby voice as she was held aloft. It was so pretty to hear her say 'Bessie;' and what else could she call Mrs Beaumont?

Bessie sat down.

'You are moved about something?'

'Yes, Mr McLaughlan, you looked so much like a picture I saw in the French Exhibition, a Danish picture.'

'I hope it was a pretty one,' he said, laughing at his own rough head, as he saw it in the glass.

'It was a lovely picture, — a sailor saving a baby from the shipwreck.'

McLaughlan shook himself into shape, then tossed Posy once more, and they played at 'shipwreck' for some time; but he was in as high spirits as the child, and Bessie saw the ring upon his finger, and felt 'perhaps good fortune will come to him also,' with a very pious wish that it might be so.

McLaughlan gave no one his address in London. Where he slept or where he passed his time was not questioned. He had taken advantage of his faith in Robert

Beaumont's lawyer, though, to have some letters conveyed under cover to him at the office, so he went there every day, and as yet no one had appeared to recognize in him but a sailor, who had some business with the lawyer. At once came the change.

'I am free!' he exclaimed; 'I believe Mrs Beaumont is right about the possession of the ring!'

'My dear fellow, moderate your voice. Who is Mrs Beaumont, pray?'

'I can buy up that fellow now, and will.'

'What fellow?' asked the lawyer.

'One Wilson; never mind, sir, it is all right. The Insurance Company have been most honourable. They are assured that I was not in the country at the time of the Daneton fire, and believe it was not malicious or of evil intent, &c. All the case is cleared up, and the thousands are ready when I go to claim them, &c., &c.'

'Sir,' said McLaughlan solemnly, 'I

will not take all the sum, but only so much as will serve to enable me to find Robert Beaumont, and set him on firm ground at Beaumont Grange.'

'That would be most impolitic!'

'How so?'

'In this way,' said the lawyer; 'you admit that you are innocent of this crime of setting your premises on fire, which was attributed to you?'

'I do.'

'Then take the money.'

'Or part of it.'

'Why a part only? that would look as if you were condoning a fraud!'

'Would it?'

'You insured for so much. Your place was burnt,—a crime laid to your charge. There was no trial, because you never appeared; some one has made all clear for you, by proving you were elsewhere when the fire took place; thus you take the money, because you are entitled to it.'

'I understand, thank you,' said Mc-
Laughlan, growing very tame; 'I will purchase Beaumont Grange out and out.'

'I think there will be no need; the
poor young man who alone kept it from
Robert Beaumont is dead.'

'Dead! when?'

'Here is the letter. I have opened it
this moment.'

'God rest his soul!' said McLaughlan,
crossing himself, an act of piety in truth
with him.

'Then I can give Robert the money to
live there?'

'Find him first,' said the phlegmatic
lawyer.

'Well, will you take *my* affairs into
your hands, as well as the Beaumonts'?'

'With pleasure, Mr McLaughlan.' The
lawyer was growing very respectful to the
square-built sailor. 'Shall you go to the
Insurance Office yourself?'

'Oh no, I think not. You can say you

have seen me; they would rather have your word than mine; and before I re-appear as I used to be, I will go one more voyage. I am more natural at present in this dress, and with the future and some prosperity, a softer time may follow!'

'I must have an address to write to you in case of need, Mr McLaughlan.'

' Of course;' and he gave two.

Having disposed of his own affairs, he felt prompted to go once more to visit Bessie and to hear her sweet voice say 'God speed you!' So he went, to find Mrs Rockingham was very ill, and was occupying Bessie; but more than that had stirred up Rudolf, who said,

'I am glad you are come; come in. I have the strangest letter from Bob.'

' Well, anything is good, to say where he is; I was just setting off to look for him.'

'Dear Rudolf,

      'Don't show this to Bessie. My mind has been quite gone for some months. I hardly write coherently yet. I had an illness of some kind, and a sort of infatuation was on me to get out of the hospital. I sent the child to you and meant to write, but nobody would let me, and they drove me mad. The weird little daughter appears to be our little sister. It seems incredible, but my father, in order to save some woman from desperation, married her.

    'I fancy my poor father is dead; the little girl bearing the name of Beaumont, and speaking English, was sent to me at Kiel, just as I intended to come home, but I fell sick, and somehow am back at Altona.

      'Yours affec.,

                 'Bob.'

    'Never mind,' said McLaughlan; 'I am going to bring him to you.'

'And this little girl?'

'I suppose I had better try to find out some particulars; one hardly likes to take a sister upon trust like that, though she is a lucky little specimen too.'

'I shall say nothing to Bessie.'

'No, better not. Now listen to me. I am a free man. No longer under fear of arrest, but free and rich, Beaumont. God bless and reward all who have been instrumental in this matter. I shall most likely never know, but a giver of good things anonymously cannot but be rewarded by God Himself.'

'I rejoice with you.'

'There was no trial, you see, for I could not tell my story.'

'Where were you?'

'I would rather not say. Some one has made it right with the Insurance, and God reward him.'

'He was just in time.'

'How?'

' I mean within the six years.'

' It is not nearly that! never mind how long or how short. Rudolf Beaumont, I shall put Robert into possession at Beaumont Grange, then we will wind up here and take Mrs Beaumont away somewhere.'

' To Rosario !'

Rudolf was full of spirits too.

Bessie and Posy came to take leave. Mrs Rockingham's accès of pain was over, and she was sleeping.

' May I kiss you, Posy ?'

' Not yet; you shall when you come back.'

He pretended to cry.

' Bessie says people do not get things at all when they cry.'

' How am I to get things, then, Posy ?'

' You must say, if you please.'

' If you please, kiss me, Posy.'

The little bright eyes danced as the great square man knelt before her, to beg for a kiss at parting. Posy relented, and sprang into his arms and kissed him again and again, so he went away gay and happy with the Scandinavian Ring, which he was to take to Robert, on his finger.

CHAPTER VII.

ALL FORLORN.

THE commercial navies of Britain swarm on every sea,—one has only to visit one of our great ports to be impressed with the magnitude of the trade of England.

In every clime under the sun she is energetically striving to extend her connections, and, by intercourse with other countries, to enrich herself.

McLaughlan sailed from Hull to the Baltic, and could acknowledge and weigh industrial commerce perhaps as well as any one; and having cast off Ireland, which has so long laboured under disadvantages, he allowed himself all the freedom and privileges of an Englishman, and gloried in her accumulated wealth.

'Ireland,' he said, ' may possess all the qualities which are prized as needful to place her at the head of civilization, but she has not, like England, the sense of natural prosperity.'

'I thought,' said a fellow-passenger, for they were talking on the deck of the steamboat, ' Ireland was going to look up.'

'She will look up to the stars—and stripes,' said an American, taking part in the conversation.

'She would be the better for a few days under water,' said a third, coming forward.

' Trample a friend when he is down!' came from another voice.

McLaughlan almost felt himself a renegade, and inclined to take up the cudgels once more for the forsaken country, till he considered it would be very like an Irishman to do so, and as futile as it must be absurd.

He paced up and down the deck in silence : experience had taught him one great lesson, the wisdom of holding his tongue.

'I cannot think,' said the friend who had begun the subject to him, ' I cannot think why Englishmen never meet without talking of poor Ireland.'

'She is the great national grievance,' said McLaughlan, smiling. ' The English always have a grievance in domestic life, as they usually have a scapegoat too ; but they do not like to parade their individual grievance, so find sympathy in abusing the sister country.'

'I have never met a real out and out Irishman yet, I mean one of those nationalists, who stick to Ireland through thick and thin.'

'And whose ideas are as variable as her climate ? ' said McLaughlan.

' Do they change, then ? '

' Do they not ? I have no tie there, but I have seen that she does not succeed.'

' That she does not.'

' They who succeed receive adulation, they who fail are abused,' said McLaughlan, ' so we rail at Ireland.   We talk of her harbours and rivers, say that her people are brave and hospitable ; but Ireland does not possess that position in the commercial world which all the qualifications her friends bestow upon her entitle one to expect.'

' Then, are the qualifications mere blarney ? '

' Very little better. She has wealth, but it is locked up ; whilst England trades upon her capital and doubles it, Ireland keeps it as a talent in a napkin, and procrastination is the thief that eats up her little interest.'

' How so ? '

' Ireland never is, but always to be,

blest,' said McLaughlan; 'they put off advantages and cry, Too late!'

'I suspect,' said the other, who was a man from Liverpool, 'Ireland is like our Birkenhead, the wrong side of the water.'

'I do not think you lock up your wealth at Birkenhead, by all accounts,' said McLaughlan, who was eager to change the subject of conversation, and not to let it drift back to Ireland, from which he had cast off, and did not mean to return.

Conversation during dinner turned on the number of Danes in London, as was but a most natural consequence, and there were several Danish merchants who were going from Hull to Copenhagen: these were very full of the great ball of the Danish residents in London, to be given that night by the Danish Ambassador to the Prince and Princess of Wales, at Willis's Rooms.

The next subject was the new sect in

the East, the Oriental Catholics, and so that meal and others passed with pleasant converse, as when men meet together who have been everywhere a rich interchange of ideas takes place.

These men were full of common sense, not too fine for every-day use, not too proud or too overbearing to be of service to each other. Most of them had, like Mc-Laughlan, received college education, and seen the benefit of it as they passed to and fro on the surface of the world.

'Educate, educate!' is the best motto for to-day. Nothing can be done without knowledge in these days, when not to know is to be left behind.

There was one man on board who was strangely out of place. He was going to Norway for sport only, and at first seemed inclined to play the cold and aristocratic, and as the American said,—

'To sit, and let the cars go by;'

but he warmed up when he found what earnest, steady-going men the merchants were, and improved his mind too by accepting a great deal of useful information which had never been set down in a guide-book.

This man singled out McLaughlan, but the latter was full of thought, and tried to spend his time in scheming for the Beaumonts; yet some hours of familiar and agreeable conversation passed between them.

' I suppose you are in the Royal Navy?' said the officer.

' No; I am not in the navy at all. I had for some time to assume a disguise, and I chose this: it suits my present expedition, and I continue it, for I am in search of a friend.'

' Is he also a naval officer?'

' I told you I am not a naval officer. My friend obtained some trifling appointment in the Library at Altona, a mere pittance, but his affairs were in a very bad condition, owing to a Bank failure, in which all his father's money was swamped.'

'I have heard Lord Dunburgher mention a similar case of one Mr Beaumont, whom he much esteems.'

'Robert Beaumont! he is the friend I am seeking now.'

'I wish you success. I am, in fact, to marry a daughter of Lord Dunburgher's next year. He makes me wait till then, so I made off to while away the time with a better sort of game than I can get in Ireland.'

'Is your place there?'

'Yes, in the county Cork.'

'You will stay for a winter in Norway, I suppose?'

'If I can; my leave will last that time, I expect; and I should like it. I want bracing up, they tell me.'

'You will get braced enough.'

'The thing is getting back.'

'Over the ice? you mean. It is no-thing to you. If you had a cattle-ship it might be a consideration. I have on some occasions known ships kept till the middle of March, and at Hull cargoes of goods waiting to come out. So you see, my lord, ice to such people is a thing of ex-treme consequence.'

'Yes; a new idea to me.'

'It is so. One half the world has totally different ideas from the other half. You have contempt for mercantile men?'

'Not contempt.'

'I am glad of it.'

'You see we have no thoughts in com-mon.'

'No; I perfectly understand. There are substances which never can amal-gamate,' said McLaughlan.

'I am not sure,' said the officer, 'that it is of any use to try.'

'Quite the reverse, it would only be waste of effort; we can all, I think, fit our minds to meet each other on neutral ground, and then each go back to our proper territory.'

'I wish you would tell me what yours is, Mr McLaughlan,' said Lord Cranbourne.

'My territory is unknown, my lord.'

'You are over-acting your part.'

'I have neither part nor land, nor home nor interest, my lord, except in these friends, the Beaumonts.'

'Forgive me.'

Lord Cranbourne noticed the deep pathos of his voice, and the light which came into his eyes now and then, only when some chord touched a remembrance.

At Copenhagen they parted.

'You will look me up at the Albemarle, Mr McLaughlan; Mr Beaumont is sure to go there to see after his friend, Lord Dunburgher.'

'Many thanks; I wish you good sport and success in life, and wife,' said Mc-

Laughlan, for the ring was on his finger, and he felt cheerfully inclined.

Robert had accepted a situation of trust in order to live, when he could not find Captain Beaumont; but with anxiety and disease came a cerebral malady, which laid him very low.

McLaughlan found him in a fair way to recover, under excellent care at Copenhagen, so having administered the best of medicines, hope, in exactly the proper quantity for sustentation, he told him to obey orders, and get well when it suited him, for that he intended to wait and amuse himself in Copenhagen till both were able to return to England together.

Helga was at her little farm in Jutland; besides, McLaughlan was shy, and did not know her except by name.

He made out a relative of the Magnusens, and learned that Captain Beaumont had gone to England in order to search for some deeds which he had left in the charge of the Danish Banking Company; that he had on departure promised to send some scientific instruments from London to Copenhagen. In due time there came out a tin box, which contained parchments only, and they had taken charge of them, expecting that Captain Beaumont would either come to claim them, and bring the instruments with him, or write a letter of instructions, but nothing more had transpired, and the cold-blooded Magnusens, as McLaugh-lan had called them in his heart, had been content to wait, and make no sign. They had not seen Robert since he took the small-pox, and were quite of opinion that Captain Beaumont had married some young woman with whom he had been seen, and that there was a little child.

These were not the Reikivig Magnusens, but only very distant relatives, and they were entirely indifferent to the interests of Robert, so McLaughlan had leave to carry away the tin box, which contained indeed the title, and all due parchments concerning Beaumont Grange.

'It must be the ring!' he said in a burst of delight, as he packed the box again and locked it, to be ready when he was, for England.

Robert, under the eyes of his friend, visibly improved. His memory returned, and his reasoning powers, which had for months deserted him.

'You were over-working, Robert,' said McLaughlan.

'I was so miserable,' he said.

'So you tried to make us all so? what was your attempt?'

Robert mentioned what he had tried to do, and how his health broke under the pressure.

'My dear fellow, your immortality would have been insured, but I do not believe the Recording Angel himself could have written so much, and not have felt it!'

'Well, do not blame me, Donald,—I was so very miserable.'

'Tell me all about it.'

'I was so out of money and low in estate, that I took the post of second librarian. You have heard all that, and how the small-pox, finding me down, cut me still lower.'

'Yes, when you sent the child home.'

'How is it?'

'Well; it is a joy to Bessie.'

'Has she no others?'

'None.'

'Poor little thing! I fancy it is our little sister; all my efforts to make anything out failed, and I fell sick, and having the little one on my hands, gave it to a stranger, with enough money to free it to London, poor little thing! Donald, do you recollect Ella Storton?'

'Yes, certainly.'

'I cannot prove what I say, but I do think that baby child is hers.'

'And — that — she — married — your father?'

'It is between you and me, this idea; but I must tell you, she asked me to marry her, but I knew she only cared for Rudolf, and was angry because he liked Bessie better. I am half sorry I said this.'

'You can trust me, Robert?'

'I can. It seems to me that, foiled and vexed, she has made the old man take her.'

'I do not believe he would.'

'Whose is the little one?'

'God knows.'

'Does Bessie know what I said to Rudolf? I told him not to tell her.'

'Neither did he. I saw your letter, though.'

'Did you? Then you are Rudolf's friend.'

'Yes, Robert, and yours. The little thing is called Posy now, and is a nice little creature. We have had enough talk for to-day.'

'Where are you going?'

'I hardly know. I am quits with the sight-seeing of Copenhagen as of other places. I shall moon about the streets, and strike up some new acquaintance in the harbour for a day or two.'

'And lay in a store of cherry brandy.'

'No, Robert; the beauty of commerce consists in the facility with which one can get anything anywhere. Good-bye.'

'Good-bye, Donald.'

Mooning, as he called it, about the streets, McLaughlan saw a little green-looking picture, of troubled water, with red lights and thick banks of cloud. Three sea-gulls gave it life, of which two were touching the dark waves.

'I wonder who painted that?' he said, for the troubled water touched him, and the soaring white gull over it.

He inquired in the shop who was the artist.

' Madame Jerichau, Monsieur.'

' Where does she live ? '

' In Thorwaldsen Street.'

And thither he proceeded.

A woman told him that Madame never saw any one.

' Which is her studio ? ' he asked.

The woman pointed, and left him to his fate. She would be blamed and dismissed; he, that great strong man, appalled her, so she went away.

McLaughlan had no idea whom to expect. He was delighted with the little picture of troubled waters, and meant to purchase it, and take it home to Bessie.

He knocked at the studio door.

' Qui est là ? '

' Ouvrez,' was his reply.

The door unbolted itself.

McLaughlan entered.

In the studio, in a thick serge gown, with a little old shawl tied in a negligent manner about her head, from which dark hair escaped, Ella Storton sat painting.

She was crouching on the steps, and did not look who it was, as she could but suppose it was her servant.

In his astonishment, McLaughlan said, ' Ella!'

He had, of course, never called her so before, but the recent conversation with Robert brought the name to his lips.

She sprang up with a wild spring, like a tigress.

'What brought you to Copenhagen?'

'I am come for you, Ella,' he said, wishing now to soothe her.

The dark eyes flashed fire.

'I choose to remain where I am! you have no right to interfere!'

'Where is your child?'

'My child is safe, thank you,' she said, very coldly.

'Do you know that Robert Beaumont is also at Copenhagen?'

'I know nothing. I care for nothing. I am dead. Why do you come?'

'To rescue you, since I am here. Ella, believe me, I did not know you were here. I came to purchase a picture I had seen, of Madame Jerichan's.'

'It was manly to intrude,' she said with bitter scorn.

'Will you forgive me?'

'I never forgive.'

She was standing now with her back to him, but he put out his hand to her; she turned fiercely towards him.

'Will you ruin me? Will you tell all the world what your eyes have seen?'

'What have my eyes seen?'

'A woman who is independent of the world! who maintains herself, who worked for a child, till it was taken from her.'

'It is well. I have seen it lately.'

'You have?'

'Yes; it is with Mrs Rudolf Beaumont. Do you know that?'

'I know nothing, except that I am

desolate; go now, you have learned enough.'

'Do you know that—'

What he was going to say was lost in a wild wrench which she gave his hand. She saw the ring, and cried,

'How did you get that?'

He told her how he had found the father, dead, at Beaumont Grange.

'Dear old man, good old man! I wondered why I never heard of him,' she said, and her variable spirit sank now into a flood of bitter tears.

'Go away now, please,' she said.

'When may I come again?'

'To-morrow, at the same hour.'

'You will not deceive me?'

'I deceive every one! do I? well, I will not deceive you. Go,' she said, and as she rose to open the door for him, and rang a bell most violently, he had no alternative.

The next day Ella received him with a quiet smile.

' You have not told all the world who I am ?' she asked.

' I have not mentioned you.'

' Thank you, sit down. I shall tell you a strange story. Have you any one to wait for you, to care for how long you are here? I do not wish to get you into trouble with your wife, if you have one.'

' I am alone in the world.'

McLaughlan's reply gave some sort of impetus to her strange nature. She did not proceed, as she had at first intended, but dawdled about the studio till he was out of patience, and told her so.

CHAPTER VIII.

MADAME JERICHAN.

'I SUPPOSE you would not tell me a story of your life?' said Ella.

'I have none to tell. None that I can tell, so go on.'

'When you came to Dancton, do you remember me?'

'Yes; Miss Storton was considered a young lady worth seeing.'

'Did you admire me?'

'I hardly know. I recollect seeing you at the Assembly Rooms, and hearing that you were engaged to Rudolf Beaumont.'

'It was not true.'

'Was it to Major Sutton?'

'No, to neither, nor to Robert Beaumont, though I liked him the best of all, but he would not look at me. I have lived to see everybody hate me. It is your turn now.'

'I shall not hate you.'

'Yes, you will. Listen to me. You came to Daneton. Robert Beaumont would not look at me. You were a little like him; and new, and of another class, and so excited my curiosity; but you were harder to attract and to deal with than even Robert Beaumont. At that ball I could not get you to see that I wished to be a friend. You resented my forward manner, and vexed me.

'I knew Mrs Beaumont so well, as to hear intimately all the news of the household. I determined to be revenged on you, and then to have you in my power. I am a poor foiled woman now, but do not pity me,—it will bruise and sting me more.'

'Very well, I say nothing; go on,—I will make no remark.'

'It was easy for me to pretend to my mother, Lady Storton, that I was to remain at St Nicholas House just at the time of the sale of things to you, but Mrs Beaumont had not asked me, so I hid myself, and waited till night, for I knew the premises well. I dressed in a coat of Robert's, but I intended to personate you, not him. I glided into her chamber and took Mrs Beaumont's Scandinavian Ring, intending her to lay the loss of it to *you*. She sprang from her bed and caught me by the wrist. With a mother's instinct, she must have recognized Robert's coat by the smell of it, —she had not light enough to see. She went all round the garden after me, and I had great difficulty to re-enter the house, and hide in the garret unseen.

'The confusion of packing let me get away to the Suttons' in time for breakfast, where a fit of sulks about Benjamin made every one so uncomfortable, that they were glad to drive me home, and my visit was never alluded to.

'It killed Mrs Beaumont, as you know, and she died, thinking that Robert had come from Oxford to take her ring.

'I intended to give it to you, but you avoided me. I was unfortunate in every attempt to meet you; and my father was not easy to manage. I got Wilson to do you all the harm I could. I wanted to rescue you, to give you the ring, to bring you to my feet, in fact!'

'A poor ignoble conquest!'

'Not so in my eyes,' said Ella.

'How came you here?'

'My mother was always delicate, and we were often at Torquay. There she died eventually, but not till I had made an ac- quaintance with Helène Magnusen, who also died after three winters spent there. She taught me what I know of the Danish tongue, and Denmark became familiar to me, so I chose it for my home, when poverty and disgrace assailed me.'

'What disgrace?'

'Every kind, actual and slanderous.'

'You talk as if reckless.'

'No; my father married the housemaid seven months after my mother's death. I am to have money at his decease. I have nothing until then from him, unless I could have lived under the pretty housemaid. Before that my life was made up, though I little thought that poverty would be added to my torment.'

''Tell me all about it,' said McLaughlan in the way he had if very much interested.

'I had a friend near Torquay, a woman friend— I will tell you the rest to-morrow,' she said, and opening the door, he, McLaughlan, went away.

Perhaps she was tired, or perhaps a regard to appearances induced her to send him away, but he went, as quietly and obediently as possible.

The next day McLaughlan was at the door of Madame Jerichan's studio, as Ella's name stood in Copenhagen.

She received him with a little bow, and sat crouching on the steps, where she had been painting.

'I hardly know why you come,' she said, without looking up.

'Nor I,' he replied, with more honesty than politeness.

She put out a very thin hand, and he took it for a moment, and said,

'Go on with your story.'

'It will only make you angry.'

'Never mind.'

'I am not good even at telling a story,' she said; 'but I shall ramble on, at the risk of offending you. I shall be then where I was—alone.

'You came to Daneton, and were the very opposite of anything I had ever seen. Rudolf was my first love, but he did not return it,—he never liked me,—I was too brusque and overbearing for him. I heard it said you were not a gentleman; my poor mother cautioned me not to dance with you. What trouble I had to get you to ask me, and you were proud and stiff, and treated me with a sort of disdain that piqued me terribly. Robert Beaumont, who was always kind to me, told me he liked you, but that his mother did not. I am repeating, but let me have my way. I meant her to think ill of you, and then I intended to throw myself into the breach and save you. I wanted to take your part; I was a wild strange girl. I stole the Scandinavian Ring, meaning to turn that to your advantage; it was a childish plan. Mrs Beaumont would not lend herself to my schemes. I stayed surreptitiously in her house, disguised in Robert's coat; I meant to be mistaken for you. I never thought of her accusing Robert; I never thought she would rise and follow me, or break her heart, and have embittered Robert's days.

'I could not meet you after her death. I was sore and vexed.

'Flirtation failed. There was one who cared something for me, but he thought my heart was gone, and he cast me off, and married another.

'I could flirt, deceive, and pretend as other women do, for a time; but the veriest automaton soon found me out,—they thought me a heartless flirt. So I was. What little heart I had was gone—unsolicited—to you. Robert Beaumont would not have me. He was a little like you, and I wanted to transfer my love to him, and be good to him, and happy.

'He was so good. I often now rejoice that I did not succeed.'

'Then I am not good, Ella?'

'No; not like Robert Beaumont. He is good enough to worship. You are great and strong, but you have human failings, and—I am not afraid of you!'

Neither of them moved.

Ella took her rest-stick and put some touches to her picture, with a calm and steady hand.

'It could not have been in any case,' McLaughlan said after some time; 'besides, you were high up in London society, and I in trade.'

'I should not have cared!'

'You say so now, for you have re-nounced the world; but had you then re-ceived its supercilious smile, you would have winced, and gone your way unheed-ing me.'

'It is not true.'

'You think so now, for suffering has purified you.'

'How do you know? others condemn me.'

'I know nothing, but I trust you.'

'Then I shall tell you everything.'

'As you please, Ella.'

She got up from her easel, went over to where he sat, and knelt before him.

'God reward you for believing in me. You are the first for very long who has not looked upon me with doubt and distrust.'

McLaughlan sat like a great stone; he let her rise, and resume her place.

'Now I will tell you,' she said. 'My mother died at Torquay, also my friend, Helène Magnusen. I was there a great deal, and had taken to painting, as an amusement, and with very good result, —it seemed to be the one thing I could do well.

'I had become very independent, would take long solitary walks, and spend my time as pleased myself; sometimes I chartered a boy to carry my drawing materials, sometimes carried them myself, and resented officious assistance, when some de-

luded gentleman tourist had the curiosity
to watch my fate.

'Four miles from Torquay was a little
cottage, and one day I sheltered there
from a thunder-shower. A woman had an
infant on her knee. I never cared for a
baby before, but that child opened its eyes
at me, and there was born within me at
that instant something I had never felt
before. The virgin mother in adoration of
her child seems akin to it. The little
creature had beautiful dark eyes, and a
friendly look in them; she was not afraid
of me, nor did she *winge* and cry, as at a
stranger.

'The rain was over, and I had to leave,
but every spare afternoon I used to walk
alone to see " my baby." I used to call it
so, and got to ask the woman " How is my
baby ?"

'One day she put the child into its
cradle, and led me to another room,
where lay upon a bed, all fresh and white,

the loveliest woman it has ever been my
lot to see. Her dark eyes gleamed upon
me, a bright smile greeted me. I could
see she was dying ; but she had no fear.

' I cared for nothing. I waited with her
for some hours. The woman who attended
the baby gave me some food; I stayed there
that night and the next, then went to my
Torquay lodgings, and came back to the
cottage to nurse her.'

' Who was she ? it was very brave of
you ! '

' She was worth it all, and all I have
suffered since ! ' Ella added, almost fiercely.
' She told me she came by the boat from
Waterford to Plymouth ; she was called
Miss Cranbourne, and her people thought
she was with a family at Torquay.'

There came a knock at the door, or
something which roused McLaughlan. He
opened it, closed it, sat down with his back
to Ella, and she went on.

' She was so beautiful lying there,—so

beautiful, so good, so loving, and so true;
she told me this:

'"Miss Storton, I was married two years
ago, at a village church in Ireland, to the
best and dearest of men. In everything
he was unfortunate, friends went against
him, money melted all away; but I loved
him, Miss Storton, with my whole soul.
He was so good. His friends—I mean
his relatives—were bad to him. I married
him privately to make him happier; but
my friends would have been distracted
had it been known.

'"Oh, how he sorrowed for me, he
wanted to release me. I burnt the certifi-
cate of marriage, and all his dear letters,
to allay his fears, which were all for my
sake. We met whenever we could, and
life was full of joy when we could be together.

'"Circumstances came which he could
neither control nor foresee. By dint of
some diplomacy I got sometimes to Dub-

lin, and once to London, to see my husband.

' " Our marriage was never suspected, and I adored him so entirely, that his name was too sacred for me ever to repeat, lest it might lead to do him harm. I longed to comfort him with my life, but it was impossible.

' " He had to leave the country. I burned every trace of our united life before his eyes, to let him go more freely, and never told him one word about my baby.

' " Of course he was not free to marry another, but he would not have done so, neither would I; but I released him, and told him he was ' free as air,' and that he must be so to please me, and he said he consented for my dear sake, and so we parted for ever—man and wife, in the sight of Heaven, strangers on earth—for evermore." '

Ella went on with her painting, McLaughlan rose, and went away.

CHAPTER IX.

SENZA SPERANZA.

MADAME JERICHAN worked at her new picture. It was a great rock, massive and tall, with waves dashing round it, and light breaking over all, as if the worst were over.

Two or three days elapsed, then the knock she had learned to listen for came again, and McLaughlan took his accustomed seat.

'Go on with your story,' he said.

And she obeyed.

'That little baby came, and from the first she tied her wedding-ring about its neck, for she would not wear it, lest it might cause remark, and she was so honourable about her husband. She told me he was blameless.

'The baby was seven months old when its mother died, in my arms. I told her it was mine, and that from henceforth I would abide by the consequences, and she shook her dear head, weakly but happily : she trusted me—as you do. She had called it Senza Speranza, and made me a request that I should get it christened. I never did; it was registered by the nurse under the name " Cranbourne." She never told me *his* name, never in all our intimacy let me find out one particular by which I might identify him. She was tenderly fond of him, and spoke of "my husband" in a touching tone of love; but she never meant me to know who he was or whither he was gone; she never intended him to see his baby, or to know he had one, lest he might feel an extra pang for her.

'The death was notified in the *Times*,

" The Honourable Anna Cranbourne, at Morcombe Cottage, near Torquay, of rapid consumption." '

' And what did you do then?' Mc-Laughlan asked.

' Sought shelter with my father, with the infant in my arms. He had married the housemaid a few days before. She told him the little one was mine. I said, " So let it be." He gave me a small sum of money, and proved that I was not an heiress, as the world had believed I was, and he promulgated the idea to get me a wealthy husband.

' My father and I were quits. I left him and came to Copenhagen.

' Once I tried to get Robert Beaumont to marry me. I told you this; he refused. By some sad accident the father found me out,—me, with the baby girl, he tended, and watched, and cherished. I could not account for it otherwise than I did. I said truly that it was the child of a dead friend

of mine, but the generosity of the world
had given it to myself, and dear old Captain
Beaumont tried to rescue me by saying he
would marry me, and call her his.'

' And did you marry him, Ella ? '

' No, of course not.'

' I thought so.'

' How was the child sent away ? '

' They made me ill, amongst them,'
she said ; ' they made it out that I was
wicked, and a woman which was a sinner,
and for that dead woman's sake I bore it.
She bore yet more for the good man she
loved.'

' How did the child get to England ? '

' I scarcely know. I tell you I fell ill;
but Captain Beaumont took it, and he put
it with some English people ; then he went
to England to look for some deeds, and did
not return. I heard in a sort of dream
that the child was gone to Bessie, and
though my jealous blood was all on fire at
first, I saw that she could shelter Senza

from the wicked world as I could never do.'

' Would you like to have her back ? '

' Of course I should. I work for her. What to me are my pictures ? what to me is the price of them ? I cost nothing to live ; I am laying by wealth for Senza.'

He left her again without farewell. A great uncouth wild form left the studio, and bore away to Robert Beaumont's.

' Are you ready to go now ? '

' Quite ready, Donald.'

So Robert and McLaughlan went on board the Copenhagen steamer, and arrived at Hull, and next in London, where at a good hotel they dined, and Donald said,

' I may leave you for an hour, and find you on my return ? '

' Oh yes ; I shall not wander away.'

McLaughlan went to Rudolf and Bessie, and told them Robert was in London, well, and that on Thursday next he was to take Senza back to Denmark, as he had found her mother.

'Then,' said Rudolf to him aside, later, 'she is not whom we suspected?'

'No, she is not.'

The next day Rudolf and Bessie met Robert, and a long conversation took place as to future plans and movements.

'I am happy; there need be no hurry,' Bessie said, glad notwithstanding to know that a change was at hand.

Robert went to look up Lord Dunburgher, and received an invitation at once to make his house his home.

McLaughlan saw the case clearly.

'You,' he said to Rudolf, 'must take your wife and Mrs Rockingham to Paris; the world need not know anything further. How can they tell how long you have been there? We need not make our friends too wise. I will take care that your family lawyer duly learns that you have married Mademoiselle Brinkmann, whose father was in the Danish Bank in Paris, and who was sent to St Thomas, and died there. Beaumont Grange is to be yours—'

'Be ours?'

'Yes; never mind why or how. You will come to it from Paris, and Madame Brinkmann with you.'

'And so cheat the world,' said Bessie, smiling, 'after all.'

'Let him arrange, Bessie. I would put my soul into McLaughlan's hands.'

'God bless you, Rudolf!' said Donald. 'Mrs Beaumont, to decide quickly is a power that comes of thought and learning and experience. A lawyer must be learned on all points, and well instructed on all subjects, that he may give the benefit of his reading in one verdict. I have come by time and circumstances to know so many things, that I can act quickly and surely.'

'So I perceive,' said Bessie gaily. 'It is a very pleasant plan of yours. It will be so nice to go to Paris after Upper Dane

Street, and to settle in a home in the country. That I cannot yet understand; but I can believe in you, Mr McLaughlan, and you are such a tried friend.'

'There! Mrs Beaumont, there! that will do. Now buy Senza some pinafores and blue ribbons, and have all ready for the move on Thursday.'

'I will,' Bessie replied.

'And the shop!' said Mr Joshua Ribbs with a gasp.

'Well, yes, the shop is a consideration. I was thinking of offering it to John Davis.'

'He deserves it,' said Bessie.

'Then let him have it.'

McLaughlan told John Davis that Mr Joshua Ribbs was suddenly called away from England, and that if he, the said John Davis, liked to consider the shop and fixtures as his at a certain sum, it might be done at once.

John Davis, anxious for his wife and family, and having the proper sum accumulated, rose to the occasion, and gratefully accepted the conditions.

'You have managed everything well for us,' said Rudolf; 'how about yourself?'

'At present I return to Copenhagen to give Speranza to her mother,' he replied, taking her second name, as Bessie noticed, and kissing the little one tenderly.

Thursday came. Robert saw Rudolf and Bessie depart, went down to Dover, indeed, with them, on the plea of aiding Mrs Rockingham, but really to give one glance to the spot where he had yet hoped to have Bessie for his own.

She waved her hand to him at the moving of the mail boat, and Robert turned away, to live in the present, and to give up the past.

He returned to town, where McLaughlan was busy with manifold affairs, and at his advice prepared to remove to Lord Dunburgher's on the following Monday, by which time his tailor had promised to turn him out fit to be seen, an important matter in a man's undertakings.

A month or two in Paris would freshen Rudolf and Bessie, and McLaughlan and the lawyer gave such orders as would ensure their comfort when they desired to take possession of Beaumont Grange.

Robert had taken a vow that he would never enter that place without Bessie, and he had made it over to her as a gift, so when Rudolf should hear of it he could never think she had come to him a dowerless bride.

Bessie was freed from the charge of Speranza, which had weighed heavily upon Robert. The little thing was quite good with the stewardess on the voyage, and was left at the hotel in high spirits after they arrived at Copenhagen, whilst McLaughlan went to look for Ella.

She looked brighter when she saw him this time: her health was much improved, and her eyes had not the hollow circles round them.

'Well,' she said, 'I see you are come back.'

'I am come back; do you welcome me?'

'Yes.'

'For myself? or because you think I have been to fetch the child?'

She blushed and said,

'For yourself. I can understand how that woman loved, who could divorce her husband for love of him.'

'Divorce him!'

'She did all she could to release him, for her love for him, and died without compromising his dear name.'

'Could you have loved thus?'

'I hardly know. I am so hard, so full of faults and flaws.'

'My poor flawed diamond.'

McLaughlan muttered the words so

low, she did not hear them. But he said aloud,

'Ella, we have seen strange things. Some lovers quarrel, and there is no redress. Some break their hearts, and there is no re-union. I have told myself there is no happiness but liberty.

'I have seen a man who was such a tyrant that he could be cruel to the woman who loved him. I have known a woman so to love as to have knelt to that tyrant, till he raised her. And even then the tyrant was more cruel again, and treated her as he would treat a hound; and she, whipped and lashed, crept to his feet and licked his hand. This man was my uncle. I have admired that woman, and scorned her by turns; but, Ella, if I could be such a villain and scoundrel as to bring a woman to my feet, once seeing her there I should adore her. I am better free, for I could not be contented with moderation

love. I have been trusted, Ella; a cold
affection I should trample under-foot, but
if I could have once more a heart to beat
for me—Ella—'

'If after all these years—' Ella began.

'What, Ella?'

'You could think me worthy—'

'My poor flawed diamond.'

'Yes, that is it. I am scratched and
imperfect, but a diamond still, for, on my
oath, I have never loved one man but you.'

'I know it.'

'You think I should be too much
trouble, too impetuous, too—'

He raised her, and folded his great
strong arms about her.

Ella sighed, and was at rest.

After some moments she looked up.

'I have no right to be here,' she said,

'Why?'

'You do not care for me; you pity me,
and are compassionate; and I have done
strange things.'

'You tried to make Robert marry you?'

'Yes; and he was so like you!'

'You are not my first love, Ella.'

'Can you love me now, a little?'

'Have I taken you into my arms?'

'You pity me because I am lonely.'

'But I am lonely too, Ella; my love is dead and buried with my youth.'

'But you are young still.'

'Will you take all I have left, Ella?'

'Do you really mean it?'

'I really mean it.'

'What if you should repent?' said Ella.

'What if I do?'

'Tell me, but do not cast me off.'

'Never fear.'

McLaughlan left abruptly, and went for the little child.

Speranza was in high delight with her pretty hood and warm pelisse. She brightened up the studio.

'How well she looks! how much she has improved!' said Ella.

'Ella, she is our child, mind; you are her mother ever and always. You will do this for me?'

'I will.'

'And we will have her christened at once.'

'By what name?'

'Lilian.'

'Very well; and you? you never let me call you by a name.'

'No; do not.'

'You must have one?'

'Never mind. I will be christened with Speranza. What will you call me?'

'Gerald.'

'Then I am Gerald.'

'I wish I could change too.'

'Be Edith.'

'So I will, and give up Ella with the past.'

'It is useless to look back; the future is before us now, Edith.'

'I have loved you very much, Gerald, but think before you take me to yourself of all that the world has said of me. I am a sort of reprobate, a woman shot out of society. I have done strange things, have written for my bread, have painted to maintain the child.'

'I do not care; you are mine now.'

'And you are not afraid?'

'To-morrow, if possible, you shall be my wife. I love you.'

'Thank you, Gerald.'

The servant brought some milk and other articles of refreshment for the child, and the three partook of a pleasant luncheon together, and in as short a time as it could possibly be accomplished, and as quietly, McLaughlan married Ella Storton, but not not till he had been duly baptized 'Gerald Donald;' but it was wise to maintain his accustomed name as well as the newly chosen one. Speranza was christened, 'Lilian McLaughlan,' and Ella, 'Edith.'

What the clergyman thought of these three baptisms preceding the marriage nobody asked, nor did McLaughlan care. He had rescued Ella.

'If I could have had you long ago,' he said, 'I might have pulled down some of your hauteur.'

'It would have been a charity; but you might have grown cold, collected, and calculating by this time: it is better as it is.'

'I think it is. I am satisfied with the present state of things. Come, Miss Mc-Laughlan; come, Lilian.'

Ella dropped on her knees beside him. She shaded her eyes, and hid her face.

'Oh, Gerald!' she exclaimed.

'My Edith, what is this?'

'It has come to me! I see it all! I

am not half nor a quarter good enough—'

'My dear, you have earned all the goodness in my nature,—you did for her what I could not do. Are you sorry to be her child's mother?'

'No, so thankful. I never thought of this. Oh, Gerald, Gerald! do not cast me off,—I will try to be worthy of her.'

'You are worthy. Get up; you have all my love, all my gratitude, and I will try to atone to you for all you have suffered.'

'That is wiped out already.'

'Do not be jealous, Edith, of a dead sad past. It is hallowed to me, as the love of an angel might be. Never refer to it if you wish to please me. To be jealous of my love for her would be to give an earthly tinge to perfect purity. I am glad, my dear, to have heard how Anna died. I met her brother a short time ago, on the deck of the Hull steamboat. You are my wife, Edith. Let your first act of obedience be to disconnect " Ella " and " Edith." '

Ella tore a paper rashly in two, and said, 'It is done; *I am Edith.*' Then she threw her arms about his neck, and kissed him, saying softly, 'I am so very, very happy; it was very good of you to come for me.'

'What shall we do with the ring?'

'It must go to Robert Beaumont,' she replied.

'Yes; we will take it to him some day, Edith, and tell him how strangely things have worked.'

'I should like to stay here a little, for I have been mistrusted, and am now so proud of everything.'

'Of Miss McLaughlan, too?'

'Yes, Gerald, very proud of her.'

'My soul will be saved now, Edith.'

'What do you mean?'

'She whom I have lost brought it into existence. I was a square walking mass of humanity when she first loved me. She drew me on to goodness, and in time

nurtured the soul she had fostered in me,
for two delicious years. It kept alive
amidst many temptations for her dear sake.
Bessie Beaumont, with her smile and loving
endurance of anything for her husband's
sake, did me good, and you, Edith, have
given your life.'

'Say no more. You have given me
Lilian. I shall go and put my sprite to
bed. You will let me paint pictures still?'

'You shall do what you like, my dear.'

'And you will stay here, then, for the
present?'

'For the present, certainly.'

Ella lingering, said,

'There was never any danger for your
soul, Gerald!'

'Child, it is as I tell you. That
woman awoke it within me. Years passed,
—she sustained it. Her divine trust in me
made me wrestle with the world. She
made me conquer by telling me I was her
plea for salvation, her prayer, her hope.

I trembled lest Heaven should spurn her for my sake; but Heaven is just.'

'Were you with her at the time of the fire?'

'I was. Why do you ask?'

'It only comes to me as things do come to a woman. I recollect she would rise and write to Lord Cranbourne, and there were letters something about a fire.'

'How do you know? tell me all.'

'I had no curiosity, I only cared for her and the baby; but letters used to come from Torquay to her. I assure you I cannot define it, but I am certain it was Lord Cranbourne who deposed that you were not at Daneton.'

'How do you know this?'

'It only comes to me. I know nothing more; but you will find it is true.'

'Then Lord Cranbourne may have guessed his sister's secret, and has guarded it.' This thought was very sweet to Mc-Laughlan, and he was glad he had met

him on his way to Copenhagen, which city
he visited before his shooting time began;
and McLaughlan was very glad he had
found and married Ella Storton.

CHAPTER X.

CYRIL.

THE news of Madame Jerichan's marriage was speedily spread from Thorwaldsen Street to others in Copenhagen,
but so many strangers visit a metropolis,
and so many weddings take place, that the
wonder does not last even nine days.

Ella had no friends; there were some
few trading acquaintances who learned
that she intended to finish the pictures
now ordered, and might possibly execute
more if she had orders, so these civilly accepted the new conditions, and Madame
and the child removed to a very nice and
comfortable apartment, and Ella did not

give that attention to the studio which she had formerly found necessary to fill up her time.

She often walked with her husband, and being seen in public with him some remains of the Magnusen family reproached themselves with their desertion of her; but Ella had grown forgiving, and with her happiness all trace of bitterness vanished.

Settled for the present, then, at Copenhagen, McLaughlan fell into a system of correspondence, and had frequent letters from Rudolf in Paris, from Robert in England, and from the family lawyer, who seemed to require his counsel on all occasions.

Rudolf wrote to Ella—

'My dear Mrs McLaughlan,

'Accept my very sincere congratulations on your marriage. I assure you we consider your husband as our good genius. We can never tell up what we

owe to him, Bessie and I. When hope
and funds were low he came to the rescue,
and I leave him to explain how he did
everything,—it is to me a mystery. We
were in a strange position, yet seemed to
fear neither detection nor annoyance.

'My wife begs to be kindly remembered
to you both.

'Yours truly,

'RUDOLF BEAUMONT.'

Bessie did not write,—it was wiser and
better not to do so. Ella understood the
motives, and acquiesced. There is a great
value in silence; a great power in not act-
ing sometimes, and there is great wisdom
in letting time go by quietly. Explana-
tions do not always satisfy; recriminations
are always vain; but 'Quieta non movere'
is a motto women seldom understand; if
they have learned it, they are wise ones.

To Donald, Rudolf said,—

'I have taken it into my head that a

great commercial treaty has been formed between you and John Davis, almost amounting to fraud. Is it not so? Tell me, you dear good fellow, where does the money come from? Bessie says it must be from you. I am not a man of business, but I am sure you are, and I hope you are not cheating yourself with the view of giving Bessie and me extra happiness. Madame Brinkmann finds the air of Paris agree with her. If we stay much longer what am I to do? Take a Boucherie Anglaise, I think.

'Robert has made over the Grange; it is ready for Bessie's acceptance. What friends I have in you and Bob! I met a man yesterday whom I knew in India; I will tell you about him some day. He also paid up a small sum I had forgotten. "All the fruits of the Scandinavian Ring," Bessie says, with her pretty superstition.

'Robert had my poor father's remains placed, as you suggested that he would, in the cemetery at Daneton, by my mother's. Old Lord Dunburgher went with him, and all the Daneton people met there who in any way had been connected with us, tradespeople and others. Robert seems to have been much affected at the respect shown.

'Sir John Storton turned up at the ceremony. He has arranged matters badly I am told with his second wife, who is a perfect Tartar, and fights for her children's rights. Benjamin Sutton was there too, he happens to be on leave; he has two sons and a daughter. His father is a martyr to gout, and the old lady is gone.

'Bessie has met some people she knew some time ago, and is very happy with them, and spoils the children in a singularly injudicious manner. If I express surprise she rewards me with one of her delicious smiles, and says "those days are over." With every kind wish, ever yours,

'RUDOLF BEAUMONT.'

Bessie was very much pleased when she heard her name mentioned by a voice she knew. She was walking with Rudolf quietly under the trees, when

' Bessie!' attracted her.

' Grace!' was her reply.

The call came from Lady Truly-bridge, who was on the way to England, where she hoped to remain for a long time.

' The Duchess and Susan,' she said, ' are at Rome.'

' Is Susan stronger?'

' Yes, but unmarried; no one seems to please her. You will come and see us, Mrs Beaumont. Have you been very long abroad?'

' Not very long,' said Bessie, with a delicate blush. She left her friend to arrange whether ' very long' meant months or years, and Rudolf was surprised to find how little it seemed to matter to any one. He resolved it thus: ' We are both old married people, and no one has any curiosity about us.'

Paris is large, and one can do as one likes there. Had McLaughlan sent them to a quiet place, or to a country town, every individual would have felt it to be his or her duty to make out how long they had been married, how many children they had or expected to have, who they were, where they came from, and where they intended to go next; and pious evangelicals would have inquired about their souls, and condemned them as ritualists when they saw them go to church regularly.

All this occurred to Bessie when, a few days after Lady Trulybridge and her pretty children were gone, Mrs Brembridge and Cyril were at the table d'hôte at their hotel.

Cyril's glass found her out in a mo_ment. He rose and went round the table to shake hands with her.

'Hallo!'

He made that exclamation on perceiving Rudolf by her side. He blinked his near-sighted eyes, and said 'Hallo!' again.

Rudolf laughed quietly and said,

'You see how it is, I think.'

'I do.'

And Major Brembridge went back to his place for dinner, and his wife bowed graciously across the table to Mrs Beaumont. Afterwards she waited for Bessie, and said,

'Come and have some tea in our salon. I heard Captain Beaumont had gone to an Estancia at Buenos Ayres. I did not know you were with him. When did you marry?'

'Oh, a long time ago,' said Bessie, with a glad smile.

The four settled themselves to drink tea, and the talkative Mrs Brembridge rattled away in the most amusing manner, and told of all the regimental changes, and what they had lately done at Brighton.

'Before that we were at the Curragh. That was not bad fun;—the best to be had in Ireland.'

'When did you leave Ireland?'

'When we were so sick of it we could not have held out much longer.'

'Where is George Harris?' Rudolf asked.

'Gone to the Cape. Beaumont, you remember that girl who promised all the eggs? She had the assurance to tell her father that Harris had proposed for her.'

'What did he do?'

'Denied it. Honest George! and so accounted for every moment, that he came off with flying colours.'

'You don't mean to say—'

'That there was an action against him? No; poor George did not deserve that! but after that girl's assurance he was so straightforward, or it might have gone hard enough with him.'

'And so George Harris is gone to the Cape?'

'Yes; but next year he is to get his majority, and marry the noble Julia, is not that her name?'

'I forget,' said Mrs Brembridge, who was confidentially stooping towards Bessie. 'She is Lord Dunburgher's second daughter, Captain Beaumont; and Lord Cranbourne is to marry the elder.' Then she went on with some discourse of much moment evidently to both herself and Bessie, and Cyril and Rudolf went out to smoke a cigar together, and to take a turn round the Palais Royal.

Mrs Brembridge knew very nice people in England, and it all came out that Bessie was the owner of Beaumont Grange, and that she hoped to pass next summer there.

Next summer! Little they thought, as they sat in the comfortable salon, that war would devastate fair Paris next summer, and that the very salon would become the refuge for wounded soldiers. They had laughed at Rochefort, had smiled over the hatred of the Parisiens for Bismarck, and had seen the Empress Eugenie, beautiful and dignified, drive in the Bois de Boulogne, or receive her guests at the Tuileries.

Poor Empress! and poor deceived Napoleon! Poor noble Paris! which has since suffered such terrible things. 'Nous avons mangé les choses inconnues; nous avons mangé notre dernière croûte,' said the letter to a friend of the writer of these pages.

The Scandinavian Ring is a romance of people, not a political essay on the government of France, but with all respect for the Teutonic race, they seem to have been most efficient and true to their character, but are singularly out of place in Paris.

Before the Teuton raid, however, Mrs Brembridge and Bessie talked agreeably in Paris.

'I hope we shall never go back to Ireland, it is so sadly changed; have you been there, Mrs Beaumont?'

'Never; and I confess that I am very much prejudiced against it.'

'You recollect at Morton Langdale how they all laughed at me, for I used to legislate for Ireland.'

'Did you?'

'You smile, Mrs Beaumont, but I do assure you I tried to influence ever so many people to do her some good.'

'And did you succeed?'

'In getting myself considered very troublesome and interfering!'

'Nothing more?'

'No, nothing more. Cyril made me give it up before we went to Newbridge; and it was as well that I did, for people said ill-natured things there of every one.'

'Is that an Irish qualification?'

'I hardly know, and hope not; but I found such cold glacial manners, and such

an under-current of gossip, that I was, I
suppose, unfortunate.'

'How did the new proprietor of whom
you told us get on ?   Did he marry ?'

'I never heard.   He was a big man in
his small village, and quite unknown beyond.'

'And the Honourable lady ?'

'Just the same,—very great in a very
small circle. I have not heard of her since ;
indeed, her affairs and quarrels did not extend beyond Newbridge. I never met any
of those people in Dublin, or heard of
them at the Curragh.'

'Then you like Dublin ?'

'Yes ; Dublin amuses me. I have been
very happy in Dublin : there are nice people, and those who have seen the world are
very nice in Ireland ; they who have lived
in a corner only are the miserable gossips,
and them we treated, as Cyril says, " with
the contempt they merit." '

'You were quite right.'

' When you get to Beaumont Grange I
hope you will ask me to visit you.'

' Will you come, Mrs Brembridge ? '

' Will you ask me ? '

' I shall be so happy to have you.'

' And Posy and Fairy.'

' With Mrs Morton Langdale, perhaps,
sometime.'

' You must not forget your friends.'

' My friends are very kind,' said Bessie,
perhaps a little stiffly, for at present she
had no wish to fill Beaumont Grange with
any one or any one's children, and the free-
and-easy Mrs Brembridge thought Bessie
had something of the northern insular
dignity, which she had managed to shake
off. However, it was all very pleasant to
see Rudolf in his proper sphere again, and
to know that prospects were bright and
the future well assured. Bessie's heart was
so full of thankfulness, she did not yet
care for the society of strangers.

She told Rudolf late in the evening

what Mrs Brembridge had said, and of her offer to visit Beaumont Grange.

'And did you repulse her, my wife? Your fear as to cheating society may be wiped away, you see.'

'I think it is well to wait a little longer,' Bessie said.

'That Mr Joshua Ribbs may settle in his grave,' said her husband. 'Bessie, the wisdom of McLaughlan shows brighter to me daily: we were so entirely out of society that our returning to it will never be observed. McLaughlan says, " Every Englishman is an island! he is quite surrounded with coldness, and you can only land if he extends a little promontory." Suppose we never observe the little piers and promontories, but go sailing round our friends and neighbours for a year or two with independent colours, and do not try to land.'

'That is just what I desire, Rudolf; I

dread a crowd of visitors, and a forced sort of intimacy.'

' You will be as reserved as the Duchess of Golden, Bessie.'

'Whom I have come to respect immensely; she is now an old and a lonely woman, but has softened very much, and Susan has grown to love her dearly. Was it not kind? The Duchess herself wrote to me when Grace told her she had seen me in Paris!'

' She could not do otherwise,' said Rudolf. 'My Bessie rescued her poor girls—'

Bessie closed his handsome lips with a kiss, and Rudolf's eyes were quite dewy as well as blue.

' Will society ever forgive,' said Bessie, with a lovely look of consciousness, ' that my children's mother earned their bread?'

' Do not make me eat my words, my wife; children, husband, friends, every one must be proud to belong to my Bessie.'

They were interrupted by a knock.

'Qui est là?'

'Cyril.'

'Enter, Cyril, then,' said Rudolf, gaily.

'My wife wants Mrs Beaumont.'

'Where?'

'In her room.   Numero dix.'

'I will go,' said Bessie, and Major Brembridge saw her safely to the door, and then came back for Rudolf.

'My dear fellow,' he said, 'your wife is not very strong at present; we must do the best we can to save her from this shock.'

'What shock?'

'Madame Brinkmann is no more.'

'Dear me! it is very sudden!'

'Yes, it is sudden, but to be expected. The dear kind lady sent for me half an hour ago, and showed me a terrible paragraph in a paper.'

'Well, what of that?' asked Rudolf.

'Just what I have to tell you; she

said, " I have sent for you, Monsieur, as you are Mr Beaumont's friend. To him you are to reveal this story, but not to my child, who has suffered so much. When I married Monsieur Brinkmann I found he had been married before, and had a son who took to evil ways when quite young; he got his father into trouble with the Bank, and but for the staunch friendship of one of the directors here in Paris we should have wanted bread. My husband was sent to St Thomas, my daughter was educated in Paris, and took a diploma at the Conservatoire; she had to subsist by her teaching, the son was cast forth, and did his best to ruin us all; lastly, under the name of Wilson he made a desultory living in London. It seems he was attached to some Danish artist whom he persecuted; he obtained her money and wearied her till he found she had married. Helga Dilke, a Danish friend of mine, has kept a watch upon him. He is dead now, and here is the account; he has always been a source of anxiety to me. I beg, sir, you will pardon me the trouble I give, be generous enough to hide this story from Bessie Beaumont—" And, my dear fellow, she turned those wonderful eyes upon me, and died.'

'Are you sure she is dead?'

'Quite sure, I regret to say. I called in the maid from the ante-room, who ran for Doctor Collum, who is in this house. He came and pronounced it "heart" at once, saying it only surprised him that she had lived so long.'

'Did he know her?'

'He has seen her here, so have I. My dear Beaumont, those bright eyes and hectic colour told me at once she was bound for elsewhere; now we must go to Doctor Collum, and see what is to be done.'

'Cyril,' said his wife, meeting him as he opened the door, 'Mrs Beaumont knows all about it; indeed, she tells me she guessed how it was when you came for her. Madame Brinkmann has been preparing to depart, she tells me, for the last two years.'

So Rudolf found Bessie standing beside the Danish mother, whose long sufferings were ended.

Bessie, a true Christian, could almost congratulate all parties on the happy change from pain to rest, and Rudolf led her away with adoration stronger than ever. Cyril was a true friend to her, and made all arrangements in the most efficient manner.

The Danish Embassy gave every token of respect, and the stoppage of the banks being over, and the Paris branch having had the name and talents of Monsieur Brinkmann expended in its service, there were many persons who came forward to testify the estimation in which the Danish lady had been held, though her life had been in poverty and obscure for many years.

Paris, with all its gaieties, is yet gorgeous in its funerals; and a great deal of black cloth and silver fringe were expected just before the war broke out.

Death was very showy in the city of Boulevards, lamps, and palaces; and a great capital ' B ' proclaimed to those spectators who chose to ask ' Whose procession is that ? ' ' Madame Brinkmann, a widow of a partner in the Danish Banking Company in the Rue de —, a décédé.'

Cyril Brembridge, who had always admired Bessie, claimed her permission to accompany Rudolf; and she was glad to have some one with her husband on the sad day *Mrs Rockingham* was buried.

After the funeral Major Brembridge went to look for Rudolf: the two men resorted to St Cloud to pass the morning, but got back for dinner,—people must dine even on days of funerals. Mrs Brembridge preferred to pass the day with Bessie, so did not appear in public.

' I never gave you the [paper,' Cyril said, ' which hastened Mrs Brinkmann's end ?'

' No, I quite forgot it. I suppose it is torn up now ?'

' No, it is in my room; come there, and have a smoke. I will show it to you.'

They both began to roll cigarettes and to smoke them, whilst Cyril sought the London paper in which the poor lady had read:

' A sad mystery of the sea.'

'.The fishing smack, "Victoria,"' Rudolf read, ' of Grinstone, arrived in port on the Doddie Bank, G. Walkington, master, on Saturday night.

'The master reports, that on the previous Wednesday morning, when about 200 miles from Hunn, he sighted to the leeward what appeared to be a small schooner in distress; but on bearing down to her he found her to be a long boat, fitted with cork, and full of water. She had compartments like a life-boat, and was upwards of 20 feet long.

'There was no name upon the boat, but he supposed her to have belonged to some steamer or large ship. She was full of water up to the corks, and painted white within and without, with a brown streak round the rim.

'When alongside, on examination three dead sailors were perceived lying aft, huddled together, and a fourth athwart in the bow, with his head hanging over the rollocks. They seemed from their dress and general appearance to be foreigners, but the bodies had been frightfully "washed about," and were in a state of decomposition, and had evidently been dead some weeks.

'On the shoulder of the fourth man, notwithstanding its condition, the letters T. F. were visible, for the rough shirt was parted, and discovered the initials burned into the discoloured flesh.

'The water-logged waif drifted on, with its ghastly cargo; the crew of the " Victoria " were shocked with the horrible sight, and were too unnerved to attend to their trawling, and the smack " Victoria " returned sooner to port in consequence, and with a comparatively small cargo.

' It is thought the sailors are Danes, and probably the fourth man was French, from the brand upon his shoulder.'

' Why French? what initials are they?' said Rudolf.

' Travaux Forcés,' said Cyril, in an under-tone.

' And do you mean that this was young Brinkmann, her step-son? that this fellow with " Travaux Forcés" burnt into his flesh could be him who caused his father's ruin?'

' It seems so; be thankful he is dead.'

' It is so terrible, poor fellow! it was bitter expiation; he made his father's life-exile, and poor Madame was prematurely aged on his account. May I send this paper to my friend McLaughlan?'

'You may do so, but not reveal the fact Madame begged us to keep secret.'

'Surely not; it would be injudicious and unnecessary.'

'Now,' said Cyril, 'would you like to return to the army and take a good staff appointment in India?'

'When? immediately?'

'No, not immediately; there will be changes before long, and if in a year or two you like to resume your military life, let me know, that's all. You will find out whether you are fit for a country gentleman very soon, or pine for the anxieties and promotions, the honours and vexations, of the service.'

'You are very good to give me time.'

'Try life at Beaumont Grange for a little at any rate, and see your son comfortably established there. We shall go back to Ireland shortly, I expect, which

Laura will not like; however, she is a wise woman, and will not expect too much. Did she ever tell you of one small place in Ireland where we were asked to attend a wedding, and the ladies in the little town expected to get the Fair, which was to take place on the same day as the marriage, put off for it?'

Rudolf smiled as he said, 'That is like the Newbridge people.'

'Except that they do not marry.'

'Did they ask it?'

'Certainly, and were surprised when told the Fair could not be altered, but that the wedding might!'

Rudolf laughed heartily.

'It is so like the conceit of those Newbridge people we knew: they think the world was made for their benefit.'

'This was not Newbridge.'

'It was in Ireland, at any rate.'

'To-morrow,' said Cyril, 'I will show you an Indian friend; now good night.'

' Good night.'

' Do you know that Laura and I are to go the day after to-morrow? '

' No, indeed! I am so sorry; going where? '

' Back to London. The Morton Langdales and others are in town, and Laura has bought clothes enough; and has tried their effect amongst her friends here.'

' I hope with pleasure and success,' said Rudolf.

' I suppose so. Some American ladies she knows appear to be satisfied. I am also. Only for your mourning you should go to some of the 'Sociables,'—they are delightful. Well, once more, good night; take this bundle of cigarettes.'

' No, thank you, I have enough. I always wind up with eau sucrée, so will come down and get it now.'

' Let me know from time to time where you are.'

' Beaumont Grange, I suppose.'

CHAPTER XI.

THE INDIAN FRIEND.

THE next day, whilst Mrs Brembridge was busy arranging for the careful removal of all her vanities and purchases in Paris, Cyril called for Rudolf to go out with him, and as they walked along the Rue de Rivoli, with a glance at the shops on the left hand and the soldiers on the right—for when was Paris so gay and so full of soldiers as a short time before the war? —it occurred to Mr Beaumont that Cyril was leading him, so he asked,

'Where are we off to?'

Before he had time for a reply, a tall man with white moustache, and a dark handsome face, came forth from the Porte cochère of one of the fashionable hotels.

'Oh, here you are!' he said, extending his hand to Cyril.

'My father, General Brembridge, Mr Beaumont.'

Hats were lifted, and the introduction made, the three turned into the gardens of the Tuileries together. Cyril looked very proud of his Indian friend.

'I worked at Paris a little yesterday, and am satisfied now, Cyril, and ready to go with you and Laura to-morrow.'

'That will be very pleasant,' said his son.

'Mr Beaumont, Cyril tells me you are his friend, his only one, he says. All the better; people do not want a multitude. I hope to be in town for a year, and shall have pleasure in seeing you as often as you please.'

'Do you go back, then, to India?'

'Yes, I expect so. I have been there

all my life, and am used to it, and except
Cyril, who is independent of me, I have
no ties in England. People are generally
crowded with relations and friends,—it is
rare for a man to come home as I do. I
had a brother—you have heard the story,
Cyril? When I first came home on leave,
he was on his way out; we met at night
in the Desert, in the days of sand and
camels, Mr Beaumont — looked at each
other by torch-light, and never met again.
He gave in to the first fever. I held out
over fifty fevers, choleras, and engage-
ments.'

'And the Mutiny, sir,' said his son.

'Yes, that has gone into print. Cyril,
I want to see the Musée de l'Artillerie. You
come too, Mr Beaumont. How do we set
about it?'

Rudolf, knowing all particulars, went
with them, and an agreeable hour or two
passed.

General Brembridge dined at the hotel

in which Cyril and Laura and the Beaumont's lived.   After he left his son said,

'Is not that a father to be proud of?'

'He is indeed,' said his friend.

'I should like very much to tell you a singular episode in his life, which was saved by a poor fellow who gave his own for him.'

'Tell me about it too, Cyril,' said Laura; 'I like that poor fellow,—he gave his life in a good cause.'

Mrs Brembridge met her father-in-law in Paris, not having seen him before, and told her husband she liked the father better than the son!

'It is quite early,' said Bessie, 'tell us the story now, Major Brembridge, whilst we are together,—it may be some time before we meet again.'

Cyril told him about a pleasant country place, of a still summer afternoon, and a young man who walked across a heath which had a lonely footpath, and a clump of fir-trees were on the summit of the highest spot, in a rather flat country.

On the left were Emstile woods, brown and tinted now with autumn, but looking very warm in the sun. The level country below could be seen for miles blue and peaceful. It was a real English picture, which Cyril drew very skilfully, and placed the locale so vividly before Bessie's eyes, that she was very much touched: it was one of her powers to see vividly what others imagined and passed.

'The young man enjoyed the landscape as much as any one could do, for he had landed within a short time in England after four months' voyage.

'Lieutenant Rawdon Brembridge had been ordered home on sick leave from India.

'It was just after he met his brother in the desert, you know,' added Cyril.

'Sallow and thin, but with health recovered, he preferred to take this walk;

the sense of strength returning was very sweet to'him; and he was on the way to pay a pleasant visit, so felt as light-hearted as when, a school-boy, he had obtained an unexpected holiday.

'He pictured to himself the happy parsonage to which he was going, how Mr Rivington would be in his study reading, and his wife going hither and thither on errands of kindness, how the young ones would welcome him, and how Emily, whom he left when fourteen, would look, with her growth and young ladyhood arrived. Wondering, too, with a pleasant flutter, whether Emily would ever be his wife; such were Rawdon Brembridge's meditations as he trod the springy turf, that bright September afternoon.

'Arrived at the highest spot, he flung himself down to enjoy the view, and to rest his long legs. He remained happy and thoughtful, till a donkey startled him into recollection, by cropping away at the grass very close to his head.

'The beast was tethered, and a small cart containing peat was near, when Rawdon got up to look about him.

'For some minutes he could find no owner for the donkey and cart,—the lame little brute had interested young Rawdon, tired of the voyage, and enjoying anything in his restored health. After a time he. discovered a lad of about seventeen fast asleep on the grass, with his cap over his eyes to shade them from the sun.

'Rawdon, struck by some power in the face, half hidden though it was, touched him gently, and the youth started up, and seemed astonished at the presence of a stranger, and a gentleman.

'In after times that face became well known to Rawdon, but even then, with the quick nature he possessed, and the observation of different races, the young man noted it as a remarkable one.

'It was squarely formed, and with a determination unusual in his rank in life. The colouring was ruddy, but the eyes when seen were dark and bright, with a wistful, longing expression, that Rawdon thought reminded him of a faithful dog. He sat up, and his keen eyes having stared at the stranger, accepted his chief points, as quickly as Rawdon had taken in his.

‘ “ Fine day, sir,” said the boy.

‘ “ Very,” said Rawdon. “ How far do you consider it to Emstile ? ”

‘ “ Two or three miles, according as you mean, the church or the street.”

‘ “ You do not belong, then, to Emstile ? ”

‘ “ We belong to nowhere ; we have neither church nor parson at Withend.”

‘ “ How do people get married or buried, then ? ” Rawdon asked.

‘ “ They have to go to the Union if they want such things, or to Ferndaleford, ever so far off, but Withend people mostly go nowhere ! ”

' " How so ? are they better than others ? "

' " Not much," the boy said, with a strange smile. " The farmers never take them except when they can get no others."

' There was something ready and frank in the boy that Rawdon took a liking for him, and went on talking, and drawing him out.

' " How do you live, then ? " he asked.

' " I do anything they give me, and help myself." He gave a glance towards the woods, to indicate that game was considered common property in those parts.

' " Does that pay like regular work ? "

' " I never tried regular work, I tell you ; the farmers never employ Withend men."

' " Would you mind telling me your name ? " Rawdon asked.

' " I am called Will Browning, and my father is known as Poaching Bill ; but we have the best of them, for we can thrash any five men of other hamlets."

' "And so," said Rawdon sadly, " so you have lived all your life?"

' "No, not all; I was with an aunt at Fernlyford till I was fourteen, but when she died I had to come here."

' There was a slight quiver in his tone as he mentioned his aunt, which Rawdon's sharp ear noticed.

' " Did you like the change?"

' " No, not at first; it was very hard."

' " Hard, was it?"

' "Very; besides, my aunt was a good woman."

' " You find it difficult to keep up what she taught you?" said Rawdon.

' " Impossible!" replied the boy.

' " Do you mean always to go on in this uncertain kind of way?" Rawdon asked, with a strange interest in his new friend, and he sat down and began to play with the grass and heather.

' "I have got now to like my liberty," he

replied candidly, "so I could not be much now; apprenticeship would be galling now."

' "I suppose it would," Rawdon remarked with equal candour. "I must be going. Where do you live? if I come here again some day could I find you?"

'The young man's face flushed with pleasure. "Anybody at Withend will show you where the Brownings live, sir. I will take care to leave word where I am gone." So the two went their ways, Will with the donkey cart, and Rawdon to Mr Rivington's.

'Withend was a terrible cluster of hovels. The fresh breeze probably prevented fever, or it must have had a home there. The most sultry day of summer felt the breeze from the common, and sometimes the cottagers pulled the rags out of the broken windows, and let a little fresh, pure air from the purple heath enter.

'Donkeys and pigs roamed at pleasure

and fed in the lanes, chickens strayed from house to house, and rough, unwashed and uncombed children quarrelled with one another.

'It was as Will had said, there was no place of worship of any kind, no church, no school; a beershop was the point of attraction, and any business was transacted there.

'The master was willing to receive any number of hares or pheasants, either in payment of old scores or in regular trading, for the Emstile woods produced good game, and the poachers were vigilant, and the keepers properly in awe of them.

'William Browning was the most daring of the Withend gang, and his sons promised to follow his example. His daughters were bold, gipsy-looking girls, able to take their own parts; his wife was a weak creature, who would have been better, but was always in fear of her family.

'A scrambling life was led of muddle

and dirt, and sometimes of poverty; but food was sometimes lavishly used, and extravagance was the Withend idea of comfort.

' Hen-roosts supplied food when game was scarce, and a fight was a legal and accustomed enjoyment; indeed, a ring to watch the combatants was no unusual gathering of the heads of families at Withend.

' To such a place Will Browning went, keeping beside his slow donkey, never trying to hurry it.

' In the afternoon's talk, a gentleman had spoken kindly to a Withend man, not with condescension, but with friendly feeling. Anything like patronage this outcast would have resented, but the face of Rawdon Brembridge had shown real feeling, and not aversion.

'Feelings and thoughts which were poor Will's at fourteen came back to his mind: his aunt had taught him a great deal of re-

ligious and other knowledge.   And he was
at fourteen a well-mannered boy, and now
this gentleman had treated him with
courtesy, and something good was roused
within him.

'The new life with its wild liberty had
something attractive to his high spirit, but
he found that his scruples were fast wear-
ing away, and on summing up, he now saw
how changed his character was. He had
become as daring as his father, and as
wild and free as any other Withend man;
yet good thoughts existed, and were ready
to break forth.

'He shuddered now at the thought of
his home,—the step-mother certain to be
beaten, the girls rash and impertinent of
tongue.

' " I suppose I shall get used to it in
time," said Will, " but if that man comes
and talks again I shall have to quit."

' Will found a fine hare ready for supper
from the Emstile woods, and some days

passed, and the gentleman did not appear.
One day he took more beer than usual,
and Will got into a violent quarrel with a
friend, and heard the landlady say, "What
can you expect of a Withend savage?" for
it was at Wolscroft, the market town, that
the quarrel began. Then came to Will,
Rawdon's words, "Do you mean always to
go on in this way?" And he strode away
to the common, to lie in the grass, and
think things over.

'The next day he was in the dirty, miserable cottage, when he heard a voice ask,
"Does Will Browning live here?"

' "Yes, sir," said Will, starting forward.

' "Good morning, Browning," said
Rawdon, in the same tone he would have
used if addressing an equal. "I am so
glad to find you at home. I have a day's
shooting in the woods, and want to find
some one to carry my bag; can you
come?"

' " Surely, sir."

' Will was ready in an instant, and brightened into a different creature; but his face very soon became overcast, and he switched at the ferns or nettles with an impatient, angry, vengeful way that made Rawdon see he was ill at ease. The headkeeper too passed them, and seeing who carried Mr Brembridge's bag, said some words of caution to Rawdon, who took them coolly, till the keeper, vexed, said,

' " Sir, I would not trust myself with him for fifty pounds."

' Will let the keeper get out of hearing, and then said, "Sir, I will leave you, if you please."

' " Nonsense, Will. I am the best judge of what company I choose to keep."

' " I am a heathen savage, sir," Will argued.

' " And why are you? "

' Will poured forth all his troubles.

' " You had better make a fresh start," said Rawdon.

' " I said so to myself yesterday. I will do so."

' " You will find it hard work, I dare say, but you can manage it."

' " Do you think so, sir? "

' " I do."

' Will got brave and hopeful, and when he went home he did a little towards putting the house in order.

' " There shall be one decent Browning," he said.

' Jeers and taunts assailed him. He went over to Mr Rivington's church, amidst manifold jests and misconstructions ; but the young lieutenant from India noticed him and said, "Good morning, Will Browning." And he saw the devoted face then turn the wistful, dog-like expression upon him.

' In April Rawdon Brembridge, having

won his Emily, was to marry, and take her out with him to India.

'Will went to see the wedding, and it was the last sight of Rawdon for some years.

'More than once he stopped Mr Rivington, and asked, "How is Mr Brembridge, sir?"

' "Very well; shall I say you asked about him?"

' "If you please, sir, when you write."

'Once the vicar added, later, "Shall I say Will Browning has not forgotten him?"

' "Do, sir, and never will forget him."

'Years passed, and Will was looked on with more respect, and his earnings became all the family had to depend upon, for one of the farmers had given him a trial, and he had given up poaching, a service of self-denial. The Browning temper was not quite dead within him,—he was a good shot, and full of energy.

' There were changes, too, about With-end. The heir had come to live at Em-stile, and Reform reared its head, and the poachers looked on Sir John Prior as their natural enemy.

' Miss Prior tried her hand about the neighbouring hamlets; but she was proud, and went about with a man-servant and a maid, for she was a little afraid of the wild inhabitants.

' Sir John took a fancy to Will Brown-ing, but Miss Prior treated every one on the defensive, especially as the good, modest young fellow treated her and the maid with rigid courtesy; he was more than once at dinner when she took her walk into Withend, and as she was over-bearing and commanded him to go to the Hall for something she had forgotten, Will had to explain that he was not his own master, but had run home for a hasty meal, as his work that day lay in a near direc-tion.

' The lady was offended.

' " You could send your man-servant, ma'am," she chose to consider interference.

' Leaving the house to return to his work, a passer-by called him " an April fool." He had forgotten that it was the first of April; but jeered upon the subject, he dashed out with his fist, and the two were fighting like savages, when Miss Prior appeared in the village street.

' The opponent was soon stunned, and Will went to his work, but Miss Prior's evidence was so exasperating that Sir John sent for Will, and began to harangue him on the subject of brawling; his farmer master, vexed at the whole affair, turned him off, and Will threw himself on the common to think, as he had done before.

' There was a girl in the neighbourhood whom he loved, and for whom he waited, hoping to work out a sort of redemption, and then ask her to take him. She met him coming from the common, and said as she passed him,

' "I wonder you are not ashamed."

' Next day it was all over the place that Will's Polly had turned him off, and was going to marry a Wolscroft tradesma n.

' Will walked away from Withend that night to find out the best way of enlisting in Rawdon's regiment, wishing heartily that he had done so long ago. In six weeks he was on the way to India in the " Arethusa."

' Eight years after we will take up the story of Will Browning, changing the pleasant English moorland to the Indian town of Adrapore, on the banks of the Ganges.

' Far as the eye can reach are rice-fields dotted with palms, and shining sheets of water, white-walled villages and mosques. The little town looks quiet enough, but within, hatred of the white man is seen in every dark man's eye: he receives him with scowls. We are in the midst of the Indian mutiny. There comes upon the ear the booming sound of the British guns.

'Strange sights for Englishmen are about. The Hindoo with his little idol presiding over his shop, the white-robed and turbaned Mahometan passing along the street.

'We go on to a low building, enclosing three sides of a square with a dwelling-house, with blinds and verandah on the fourth side.

'The house is darkened as much as it can be, and at the same time is arranged to allow a free current of air. The sun is the enemy in India, who must be kept out. But the heat does not keep everybody within; the dark-skinned figures in white uniform move about in the blaze of sun-shine.

'The inside of the house feels cool in

comparison, but is so dark, that at first you can distinguish nothing.

'Your eyes become accustomed, then you see a bare little furnished room, a table, two chairs, a few books, a sword, some fire-arms, &c.

'At the table sits a sallow man; you watch him measuring distances on a plan or map, and must be told that he is Rawdon Brembridge whom you saw on the common by the Emstile woods that fine September day, years ago. He has grown a beard, and is a man of care and anxiety now.

'He is Rawdon—Major Brembridge, and the bronzed, matured, tall fellow by his side is Will Browning, whom we knew at Withend.

'Both look like Englishmen, whose decision it would be dangerous to alter, and whom neither storm nor shot nor shell could keep from the path of duty.

'Rawdon, left in command of a division

of his regiment, had retained it since the
beginning of the mutiny, and though his
men were disaffected, his strong resolve
and iron will had so far prevented an outbreak.

'He and Will Browning were the only
Europeans in Adrapore. Every morning
it seemed probable that both would be
killed before night.

'Rawdon's wife and children had been
sent from Adrapore to Calcutta, as the
little girls were not in good health. He
was thankful they were safe.

'For himself, my father,' Cyril said,
'waited with quiet trust either life or
death, as it should please God.

' "How far do you think they are,
sir?" Will asked of Rawdon.

' "About a hundred miles. No hope
yet, Browning."

'Major Brembridge leaned on his chair
and sighed. Will looked at the rifle he

held, saying thoughtfully, "We've kept up so long, sir, I don't see but we may keep up—till then."

' "I doubt it. Every day they are more reluctant to obey orders. If it were not for the importance of keeping this station till Outram comes up, I should say the sooner they mutinied the better. I am tired of it."

' " But the lady and the children, sir ? "

' " The odds are against my seeing them again. I have one chance only in a hundred."

' " You want sleep, sir, and are low. I'll watch ; lie down and sleep. You may trust me."

' The sensible advice was wisely followed. In a few minutes Rawdon was fast asleep. Will watched, and saw the careworn expression fade away, and Major Brembridge looked younger by years.

' " He sleeps like a child ! " said the faithful Will.

' He saw a dark face peering in between the blind and the wall. Will raised his pistol and the dark face vanished.

' " That means mischief," said Browning to himself. " No doubt he came to see if we were watching, but he will not try again."

' Will sat down to read quietly, where he could also watch by Rawdon's side.

' After some hours only he called him ; it was time for the muster-call.

' To those two men it was almost like giving the signal for their own execution, so great were the chances against them ; but they never faltered in their duty.

' This evening Browning was sorry to have to awake Rawdon, and the weary look returned to his face.

' The white-clad men fell into lines as the muster-call was sounded. There was a grin or malignant scowl upon the faces of all, but beyond a tardiness in obeying the words of command there was no indication of dissatisfaction : they wished to show they were their own masters.

' Suddenly one man raised his piece and fired at Rawdon. The ball wounded him in the shoulder ; he staggered, but did not fall.

' Will Browning watched the hands of the others moving towards the triggers of their guns, and he knew there was but one thing to be done. Instantaneously Will walked up to the man who had fired and shot him dead.

' There fell a stillness upon all. My father broke it,' said Cyril, proudly.

' " Men," he said, " you are seventy-six to two of us. It is in your power to kill us ; but I have a six-barrelled revolver, so has Browning, so we can each shoot six a piece of you before we yield our lives.

' " Stand at ease ! "

' Then he and Browning moved into the house to look to the wound, luckily but a slight one.

'Will Browning heaved a sigh of relief as he arranged my father's room for
the night, and prepared to watch beside
him, for he had persuaded him that rest
and sleep were needed to get his wound
healed.

'He thought of former days, and how
he and my father had met on the common,
and wondered what Withend had become,
since he could not but hope the heathens
and savages of the period he alluded to
must surely have vanished.

'There were no painful memories in
his Indian life. Full occupation had filled
his vigorous life, and month after month
had followed with satisfaction.

'He had at once taken his station with
the steady ones in the regiment, and it
had never been forfeited, as the good conduct stripes on his arm showed. Mrs
Brembridge had been pleased at his coming
out to her husband, and felt glad to have
an Englishman upon whom she could de-

pend. The two boys and two little girls treated him almost as one of the family, and Mrs Brembridge had said when she left for Calcutta,

'"I do not mind half so much leaving my husband, Will, for you are sure to take care of him for me."

'The long night came to an end. Browning went with the morning to fetch water for their needs during the day. He came back with a smile on his face.

'"We shall not be shot for a day or two, sir. I met Ali coming up with the last barrel of gunpowder from the stores, and just in the passage near the well I managed to knock it out of his hand, and the water too, into the powder. There was hardly any of it left dry, and that I trode into the ground."

'Rawdon's solemn face relaxed into a smile too.

'"How little I thought a month ago that I should be alive now!" he said.

" You have done well, Browning. I shall not forget it." He laid his hand upon Will's arm.

' Both the men seemed ashamed to put into words what they both felt.

' In the evening the company were mustered and dismissed, and again Rawdon and Will sat together.

' "Did you hear anything, Will?" said my father suddenly.

' Will did not.

' " My fancy is strong; I could swear I hear our old band playing!" Rawdon rose—stood—waited—listened—*heard* the throb of the distant drum; then a shrill fife note fell upon their ears, and they knew it was the English band.

' Major Brembridge was very pale.

' " I shall see them again, thank God," he said, and he fell on the sofa and waited. There were tears in the eyes of Rawdon and of Will.

'Very few words were spoken; both their hearts were so full.

'Could the mutineers be playing "God save the Queen!" in derision? The thought was torturing them both. Or could they give up these two as dead, or especially Rawdon, and march on past Adrapore?

'The music became louder, and nearer came relief, and General Outram entered the little town, happy to find the English flag still flying over it.

'My father was greeted as a hero by all the British force, and as for Will, everybody shook hands with him and complimented him upon his gallant doings.

'It was quite a new sensation to rise in the morning without fear of being massacred before night; and these two started at every unusual sound, not half aware of the strain under which they had lived lately.

'Day after day the British force marched on all through the fearful heat of that Indian summer.   All as one man pressed forward to save the women and children who were immured in the beleaguered city of Lucknow.   Along hot dry roads they went, and sometimes through country that was like a sandy desert, but sometimes through rich and fertile portions of indigo fields and flowering sugar-canes.

'Late one evening, when the sun had just set in the quick way which astonishes the Britishers till they get used to it, for they are accustomed to our twilights, they were marching by a road which had been made through a jungle.   Thick trees were on either side, up which, as you know, Rudolf, flowering creepers twine, and make a barrier ; but here and there was an opening to the river.   At one of the turns of the road an Indian girl was standing with a baby in her arms.

' Browning happening to be the last

man, saw her and recognized her. She was
the daughter of one of Rawdon's native
soldiers, and Mrs Brembridge had been
very good to her, and had nursed her
during an illness. Will remembered her
face ; but astonished as he was to see her,
he had to march on, and soon forgot her.

'An accident occurred to one of the
gun carriages, and the last division, in
which were my father and Will Browning,
were ordered to halt whilst it was repaired.

'The rest of the troops marched forward.
As soon as they were out of sight a party
of Sepoys burst upon Major Brembridge's
party, with yells and cries. A few minutes'
sharp fighting followed, and the enemy
was repulsed.

'Any who were hurt or wounded were
sought for as well as the darkness would
permit, but it was not till the next general
halt that it was discovered how many were
missing, and that Major Brembridge and
Private William Browning were amongst

them. Will had been struck down almost at the first. Rawdon saw him fall, and with a few others had rushed to save him, but they were overpowered by numbers. Three or four were killed; my father received some wounds, and lay on the ground without consciousness.

'The chief struggle was going on a that little further still, and so it happened they who sought for the wounded did not seek far enough to find my father and poor Will.

'My father, who was stunned, came to himself, and hearing no sound, struck a light and shaded it with his hand. It lit up what he wanted to see, the faces of those who were lying on the ground: he looked at his comrades, and finding them dead, got up and most joyfully met Will, wounded also, but though both did but groan—both lived.

'My father, weak with loss of blood, fainted into Browning's arms. What was to be done with a fainting man in the enemy's country?

'If Major Brembridge had not required him, Will could easily have escaped; with three or four hours of quick walking he could have come up with the army; but here he was with the man he cared for fainting, and shelter not likely to be found.

'If they remained where they were death was certain, for the Sepoys would find them in the morning, and put an end to all uncertainty as to their fate.

'Suddenly Browning thought of the Indian girl whom he had seen at the door of a hut in the jungle.

'He retraced his steps, carrying my father in the best way his heavy weight would allow, and as gently as he could.

'Arrived at the hut, he knocked softly at the door; the woman he had seen, put her face out of the window. She said her husband was away, but would return before next day.

'After a little parley, for she was afraid to give assistance, Browning succeeded in reminding her of Mrs Brembridge's kindness, and she showed them an outhouse where they could remain for the night.

'She brought straw, and some soothing application for the wounds.

'With the earliest dawn Will started into consciousness, and examined my father's condition. He was very weak, so Will persuaded him not to try to move. Suddenly the door of the shed opened, and two dark faces peeped in; they were the young woman's husband and another man.

'The woman ran down to explain who they were, and her husband listened, but the other man defied them by his glance, and William Browning recollected him as a deadly enemy to the white race.

'He pressed upon the husband the necessity for barring the door and window, lest the prisoners should escape, and said that he was going off for a guard of soldiers to secure them.

'Before long he departed, observing that he himself would have despatched the Englishman, only they had ten more lives than Mussulmans, or rather Mahometans.

'Every one felt relieved at the man's departure. The husband begged of Browning not to shoot him if he came to the window, for he had something to say.

'He said he was sorry for the position in which he found himself, but that the man who was gone was powerful amongst the rebels, and if they escaped he should be shot.

'The poor young woman sat on the ground in a sad plight, having to choose between the life of the prisoners or her husband. Browning looked at Rawdon, who had feebly listened, but failed to understand the rapid Hindustanee.

'Will said in a low voice to the husband, " Could you not save *him* without me ?"

'The dark man started; the idea had not occurred to him. The wife's quicker intellect seized upon it. The Sahib is sick. What could be easier than to say he had died, that they had thrown his body into the river? thus they might conceal him till he recovered.

' The woman repeated the plan, till her husband was convinced.

' Yet Browning's self-devotion seemed incredible to the Hindoo, and he said to Will,—

' " Can I trust you? should you not escape ?"

' " I give you my word I will not escape if you will save *him*."

' The Hindoo consented.

' " But," Will bargained, " you must not let him know; let *him* believe you can save us both."

' The woman bending over my father, said,

' " Come, I will take you and hide you till you get well."

' " I will go anywhere William Browning pleases, provided he runs no risk on my account; I heard something, but am unable to recollect what."

' " As to risk, sir, we are always in risks," said Browning ; " let us get you into the litter,—there will be less risk for you that way."

' " Can you trust these people, Will ? "

' " I think, sir, they are grateful, and would like to show that they are so, to dear Mrs Brembridge. I cannot be thankful enough that I happened to notice the woman at the hut last night."

' Rawdon lay on a heap of straw, and weak as he was, he could notice a great change in Browning's tone,—it was sad, serious, devoted.

' The rough litter came. Rawdon was

lifted in it, and carried to the house. Will saw the woman's arrangements for his comfort, and sat down by his feet.

‘The guard of soldiers could not come for some hours, so his time was yet his own.

‘It must have been a strange though hardly a new sensation to poor tried Browning that this really was his last night on earth. His doom with the rebels was certain.

‘The love of life was strong, but he could find no plea for escape now. He was bound by parole of honour to the woman's husband, and he could not leave his friend to perish.

‘He wished Rawdon not to know as yet, but he would write a letter to be delivered some time, if explanation were needed, after his death.

‘The woman procured writing materials, and he wrote whilst Rawdon slept—

" DEAR AND HONOURED SIR,

" When you read this all will be clear in my conduct. I did not wish to leave you for my own safety.

" Your life, sir, is worth ten of mine; you can believe I did not let you know, lest you should not consent. For myself, I trust in God's mercy. He will take care of my soul. You did everything for me, sir, when you first led me to seek the right way. I hope Mrs Brembridge will be well and glad to see you; she will not forget one who owed his whole welfare to you.

" Your faithful servant,

" WILL BROWNING."

' Having written the letter, Browning hid his face. A mother could not have watched more tenderly till Rawdon awoke, weak and half delirious, complaining that Will had left him.

' Browning soothed him till he got calm.

' " Can you trust me, sir, even though appearances may be against me ? "

' " I could not distrust you, Will."

' " Then, sir, it is expedient for me to leave you to-night. The woman and her husband cannot hide me too."

' Rawdon looked troubled.

' " You are right," he said ; " escape by all means; reach the British army, and you can get help. Do not remain in danger because of me."

' " It is not that, sir. Say, ' God bless you!' before I go." Will's hand quivered : it shook the bed on which my father lay, he recollected afterwards.

' " God bless you, Browning, and re-ward you, my good fellow ! "

' Will went back to his prison in the outhouse. The Hindoo said,

' " Think better of it. You are full of health; let me give the sick Sahib up,— he will most likely die in a few days."

' " Can you save us both ? "

' " No, one must die."

' " Then take care of *him*. I die."

' Browning slept for an hour or two. He watched from a loophole in the out-house then, and saw the sun rise, and was soon roused by a band of dark Sepoys, who claimed the victim.

' " There is only one; the other was sick, and is dead; we cast his body into the river," the Hindoo said.

' The Sepoy chief looked keenly at him, then ordered Browning to be fettered, and taken away by the soldiers.

' The Hindoo pondered over the devotion of this English soldier, as he repeated, " The other died of wounds yesterday, and this will take his doom quietly."

' At sunset the drum beat in the Indian camp, and the rebels were mustered. Dark faces all, round one grave white one.

' William Browning was led out to be shot.

' Gleaming swords, yells, and grins

made no impression on the devoted friend.

'His eyes faced the red glow of the sky, but his thoughts were gone to a more beautiful country.

'The cowardly savages did not end his misery at once, but kept him in torture for an hour, and then—shot him.'

'Oh, Cyril!' cried Laura from her tears, 'what a delightful, sad, horrible story! I was going to ask, Did your father recover?' she added, with a little hysterical laugh. 'How long was he with that Indian woman?'

'About two months. She nursed him faithfully, and then he was sent to Calcutta to my mother and me. The poor little girl and my little brother were gone; but my mother had not expected to see him again, so was comforted when he arrived.

'He was very grave and sad, and her wifely wisdom soon found there was more than the loss of his baby children to affect him, so she asked him what oppressed him.

' " I have lost a dear friend, Emily."

' " Any one I knew ? "

' " Will Browning."

' " Poor fellow ! " said my mother.

' " He was a hero, Emily; he saved my life at the expense of his own."

' My mother was very much affected, as you may believe.'

' Did she die in India ? ' said Bessie.

' No; she came home in delicate health, and died in England; that is why my father does not care for the country; indeed the plains of India are more congenial to him, and I think the unburied bones of Will Browning are more to him than glory, too.'

' I do not wonder you almost worship your father,' Laura said; ' he is the very handsomest, noblest, nicest, dearest old general in all the world ! '

' My dear Laura, be quiet, it is getting late. Come, Beaumont, the gas is off, I suspect, in the salle à manger, we shall get our cigarettes and eau sucrée by the light of a slender bougie. Go to bed, Laura, in order to look well to travel with your General to-morrow.

'Poor Will Browning! his being true to death in that way seems to cast extra glory on that terrible time of trial. It is a good story you have told us, Cyril.'

Rudolf put out his hand to take leave, for the General and Major and Mrs Brembridge were to be off by the morning train, and Laura wished him and Bessie a very friendly and affectionate farewell.

CHAPTER XII.

A FEW MONTHS LATER.

M^cLAUGHLAN made John Davis' fortune by handing over to him some experiences in the Joint-stock Company in which he, McLaughlan, had found his money increase. He had looked ahead, and tried to establish something in Ireland, but no one would listen: the very aristocratic idea that to trade with one's money is not for gentlemen, induced them to despise such overtures.

In vain McLaughlan wrote to them and sought to prove that it benefits the community to distribute wealth and prosperity.

In England, therefore, he set up his

scheme; and where men are alike conversant with business and with the Houses of Parliament, meetings for commercial purposes are understood, well regulated offices are kept, money is invested, and confidence inspired.

Many such are practically at work in England, where people's aristocracy does not tend to prevent their doing good to themselves and the country.

Novelists and penny-a-liners have drawn horrible descriptions of collapsed joint-stock companies, and to expose those who are unfaithful to a trust reposed may be fair enough; but do such harrowing pictures militate against commerce? If so, it is to be deplored, for it is well to encourage industry, and to help one another.

McLaughlan claimed for his, evenhanded justice and fair play, which must be accorded in all mercantile transactions; and so, according with the natural laws of trading increase, his speculation, no longer regarded as a miracle, became a substantial money-making fact.

'Poor Ireland! left in the rear again! She is not up to the idea of a company granting full provisions of limited liability; strike her out,—we must go on withouther,' McLaughlan said, and his money accumulated and doubled, and he longed to be in activity again, but consented to his wife's wish to remain in Denmark till she had finished the pictures ordered from *Madame Jerichan.*

The ravens are not fed without labour on their part. 'He that worketh not, neither shall he eat,' says the highest authority; and when Jupiter was appealed to by the carter, he told him to whip up his horses, and put his shoulder to the wheel, no other assistance being vouchsafed. Instead of folding his arms in despair, and cursing the gods, the carter tried the good advice.

McLaughlan, trained to industry, found

means by correspondence, however, to keep matters going ; and having able coadjutors in John Davis and others in London, he could afford to stay at Copenhagen for this period, during which his uncle died, the Baron Charles McLaughlan.

It turned out as Donald had suspected, that the two nephews were his sons, born, as was now seen, before the poor Baroness came to her honours.

'It is all a sad story,' said McLaughlan. 'I am glad now that I am so far away as not to have to appear at his funeral. I will not go near the place nor interfere in any way.'

'But you are the Baron now, under the circumstances,' said his wife.

'The Baron!' said McLaughlan with disdain. 'Go on with your book, and get it done as well as your pictures.'

'Oh, my book only occupies whilst the colours dry,' said Edith shyly.

'And what have you added to-day ?'

' You make me feel like that advice of the man in " Pickwick," who said, " Now don't be a poet!"'

' You say you are not one,' said her husband.

' Nor am I. I only translate into Danish some things which lend themselves to the language; and I mean to leave a little volume as a remembrance to the few kind people I have known here, and I mean, Gerald, since your uncle's death has come in time, to give my name in full on the title-page.'

' Well, what else would you put?'

' I mean my new name, my name of to-day. I shall put " Translated from English to the Danish tongue, by the Baroness McLaughlan."

' So, so! It is Madame la Baronne now. I never thought of that!'

' No, Gerald, but the world is as the world is. Madame la Baronne can do what honest Mrs McLaughlan could never have done.'

'How, my dear?'

'Take my place again.'

'Your place is with me.'

McLaughlan spoke gruffly, but he saw Ella was right.

She went on with her translation, taking, as she said, such poetry as would lend itself to the language.

Donald had a volume of poems which entranced him. He could not sympathize with 'wounded daisies,' he said, so he finished Dante Gabriel Rosetti's 'Blessed Damoselle'—he 'heard her tears,' then shook himself, and went out.

Ella wrote till evening at her Danish verses. It was a work which occupied her mind very happily.

THE WOUNDED DAISY.

At twilight in beautiful summers,
When all the dew is shed,
And all the singers and hummers
Are safe at home in bed,
In many a nook of the meadows
Fairies may linger and lurk:

Look under the leafy shadows,
    Perhaps you'll see them at work.

Perhaps you may see them swinging
    On see-saw reeds in the dell,
Perhaps you may hear them ringing
    The sweet little heather bell,
Or setting the lilies stately
    Before they begin to grow,
Or getting the rosebuds really
    Before it is time to blow.

A fairy was mending a daisy
    Which some one had torn in half;
Her sisters all thought her crazy,
    And only began to laugh.
They showed her scores by the hedges,
    And scores that grew by the tarn,
The fairy cared not for the hedges,
    And only went on with her darn.

She worked and she sang a ditty,
    While insects wondered and heard;
They knew by the tone of pity
    The song was not from a bird:
'Daisy, somebody hurt you!
    Are you frightened at me?
Patient hope is a virtue,
    Wait, and you shall see.

'Was it a careless mower
    Cut your blossom in twain?
I hope his hand will be slower
    When he seizes his scythe again.

Was it a step unheeding ?
  Or was it a stormy gale ?
Or was it—your heart is bleeding—
  By a dark malicious snail ? ·

' They did not know how you suffer:
  I think they had never seen
A delicate thing, and are rougher,
  These slugs, perhaps, than they seem.
Hush ! there is some one sobbing
  Just down there by my foot;
Daisy, your heart is throbbing
  Down in your poor little root.

' Daisy, you were so merry
  Where you modestly grew.
Earth was generous—very ;
  Heaven was pleasant for you.
Never annoying your neighbour,
  Neither too forward nor slack—
Do you not feel, as I labour,
  Some of your joy come back ?

' Ah ! you tremble a little ;
  Have I, too, hurt you at last ?
If you were not too brittle
  I could mend you fast.
No, there is nothing distrustful,
  Only a quiver of bliss.
Daisy ! I am successful,
  So now you must give me a kiss.

' Now I have mended you neatly,
  As all the fairies can see ;

Now you will look up sweetly,
    And gratefully smile on me.
I can go hiding behind you—
    Then in a day or two
Perhaps a baby may find you,
    And I may hear it coo!

' Yes, your cheeks may be whiter
    Than all the rest of your race;
Other eyes may be brighter,
    Others fairer in face;
But no flower that uncloses
    Can be as precious as you;
No, not an army of roses
    Fighting all the year through.'

All the fairies confess it,
    As that daisy revives;
They come around to caress it,
    Every one glad it lives.
No one ventures to doubt it:
    Hosts of penitent fays
Make their dance-rings round it,
    Sing their songs in its praise.

Hours of fading and growing
    Pass—the daisy is not!
Sweeter grass blooms are glowing
    Still by the little spot.
There each fairy that hovered
    Sung whilst passing above—
' Here a daisy recovered!
    Here is a footprint of love!'

Lilian highly approved of the story of the daisy, and her pretty suggestions, as she had picked up Danish quite fluently now, aided Ella in her versification, for she wanted the simplest terms.

The book was to be her parting gift to Denmark, which had sheltered her when England had been too unkind. Her last pages contained

THE SLEEP.

Of all the thoughts of God that are
Borne inward into souls afar,
　　Along the Psalmist's music deep,
Now tell me if there any is,
For gift or grace surpassing this—
　　' He giveth His beloved sleep.'

What would we give to our beloved ?
The hero's heart to be unmoved ?
　　The poet's star-tuned harp to sweep ?
The patriot's voice to teach and rouse ?
The monarch's crown to light the brows ?—
　　' He giveth His beloved sleep.'

What do we give to our beloved ?
A little faith all undisproved,
　　A little dust to oversweep,

And bitter memories to make
The whole earth blasted for our sake—
   ' He giveth His beloved sleep.'

' Soft, soft, beloved,' we often say,
We have no time to charm away
   Sad dreams that through the eyelids creep ;
But never doleful dream again
Shall break the happy slumber when
   ' He giveth His beloved sleep.'

Oh, earth so full of dreary noises !
Oh, men with wailing in your voices !
   Oh, delved gold which toilers heap !
Oh, strife and curse that o'er it fall !
God can strike silence through it all—
   ' He giveth His beloved sleep.'

His dews drop mutely on the hill,
His cloud above it saileth still,
   Though on its slope men sow and reap.
More softly than the dew is shed,
Or cloud is floated overhead,
   ' He giveth His beloved sleep.'

Ay, men may wonder while they scan
A living, thinking, feeling man,
   Confirmed in such a rest to keep ;
But angels say, and through the word,
I think their happy smile is heard—
   ' He giveth His beloved sleep.'

For me, my heart that erst did go
Most like a child tired at a show,
   That sees through tears the mummers leap,

Would now its wearied vision close,
Would, child-like, on His love repose,
 Who, giveth His beloved sleep.'

And friends, dear friends, when it shall be
That this low breath is gone from me,
 And round my bier ye come to weep,
Let one, most loving of you all,
Say, ' Not a tear for her must fall '—
 ' He giveth His beloved sleep.'

Busy with her poetry, happy with her husband, and gay with her child, for so she called Lilian, Ella finished her Danish pictures, and put away her palettes and brushes with a sort of foreknowledge that if they were ever used again, it would be in some distant country as yet unrevealed to her.

Rudolf, from Paris, wrote to McLaughlan about the death of Bessie's mother; and free and open with him on all subjects, he told that the death of Wilson had accelerated her end, and sent the paper in which she had seen the account.

Edith never inquired about any letters

which came to her husband,—she had not yet freed herself of an objection to ask anything; she felt as if under an obligation to him, in fact, so did not seek intimacy as to his pursuits or employments.

An English newspaper, however, she felt at liberty to look at, and she read the one sent from Paris, and found the paragraph marked, 'A sad mystery of the sea.

She read the mystery, and replaced the paper in McLaughlan's private room, and was very silent for some time. When Lilian was gone to bed, and a quiet hour was upon her, she said,

'You never asked me, Gerald, where the money was about which I boasted to you that I had gained, that I had worked for; did you ever wonder where it is?'

'No; never mind. We do not want it.'

'I lent it, Gerald; it has vanished.'

'So much the better; you cannot boast of it again.'

'You *will* not doubt me?'

' Why should I ? '

' Every one else did.'

' I am no one else,' said McLaughlan ;
' but if you would be happier to tell me,
do so.'

' I think I should, Gerald.'

' You are mine, Edith ; I want neither
explanation nor money.'

' Being yours, I want to stand clear.
It was to Wilson that I lent my savings,
and he was a Dane.'

' A Dane, was he ? '

' He told me his father was a director
or something in a bank, who married when
he was yet a very young man. He appears to have been wild and unsteady, and
his father cast him off after some crime.
Money ran through his fingers. At last he
committed some breach of society which
caused him to be sent to Toulon. He
managed to escape, and lived for some
time in France, but got to London at last.
His father was under suspicion on his ac-

count, but cleared himself with some trouble.

'Wilson got employment in a picture-shop. He spoke English quite well, and I became acquainted with him when I wanted to get my pictures known and sold. Wilson, however, under one plea or another, obtained my hoard from me.'

'How did you get rid of him at last?'

'By asking to be repaid.'

'That was one way!' said McLaughlan.

'Yes; I asked him for money which I knew he could not pay, but it had the effect of keeping him away.'

'Did he care for you, Edith?'

'He pretended to do so, and seemed to do so.'

'And you were sorry for him?'

'I was very sorry for him.'

'Did he follow you to Denmark?'

'He came to Copenhagen, and I met him. I do not think he knew where I was; but the persecution was harder to bear here, and I told Mr Beaumont about it. I had told him as much as I could about Lilian, and he offered to take me with my debts and encumbrances, but of course I would not let him.'

' You were right, my dear.'

' Wilson left when Mr Beaumont did, but I saw him afterwards. He told me he went with the child to England, but he could not go with her beyond Hull; that Robert had given an address to the captain of the steamer. He—Wilson—acted as steward on that voyage, during the illness of the actual steward, and thus had the opportunity of seeing the little one, who thought he was the captain. He came to tell me of the safety of the child. I declare to you, Gerald, he told me all on the steps outside the studio door.'

' Never mind, child; go on,—tell me all about it,' McLaughlan said.

' I gave him all I had; he had been kind to my baby. He said he was going from Copenhagen by the " Trologen " to Bergen.

' The " Trologen " was wrecked, and a Norwegian brig, bound to Galatz, with coals from Shields, picked up several of the crew. Now I know what became of the rest. I had a paper with the wreck of the " Trologen," and I put it into verse for some of the aching hearts. It said a boat was drifting away, and no trace of the vessel was to be seen when day broke on the following morning. So they thought she went to pieces with the loss of all left on board.'

' Was that the newspaper or the poetical version ? '

' Both. I related the facts.'

' Well, my dear, is that all ? '

' Gerald, to-day I read in a paper some one sent to you of a man with a brand on his shoulder. That was Wilson !—the dates coincide.'

' God rest his soul ! '

McLaughlan made the sign of the cross, and Wilson was blotted out for ever from his mind.

In about a fortnight the mails had brought very important news to Mr McLaughlan. He said to himself, ' I begin to believe in Mrs Beaumont's assertion, that good luck attends the possession of the Scandinavian Ring.'

In the first place, a will made by his father was found secreted amongst the late Baron's effects, by which Donald became possessed of all his father's property. It turned out to be all that the Baron had been able to use to live upon, his own share having been mortgaged and re-mortgaged; in fact, the Baron had held a false position through life, and being a skilful hypocrite, though things were surmised, people were slow to pronounce against a man without proof.

' God forgive him, as I do,' was all his

nephew said, and dismissed him.

For the two sons he provided ample means, and sent them to Canada under the most favourable auspices.

The mother had laid down her cares a few months after McLaughlan left Ireland for the last time; but he had not heard of her death during his wanderings.

McLaughlan, who plays a most difficult part in this drama, (for he sometimes speaks for himself, and sometimes has to stand aside and let the chorus tell his thoughts and doings, but he does not aspire to perfection, but rather humbly puts in a plea for a very faulty rôle and romance)—

McLaughlan waited till the return of one more mail, and then said to his wife, 'Now, my dear, if your translations are finished, I am going to translate you.'

'To Ireland, Gerald?'

'No, not to Ireland. Let Ireland respect her capabilities, and improve her condition. There is no panacea for Ireland as yet. Apathy and indolence must be driven out by well-directed energy; and the worse than unwillingness of the Irish landlords and great proprietors to encourage the development of the country's resources, must be quenched by English capitalists and progress. Then, Edith, the tide set in the right direction, we may return.'

' Return ? '

' Yes; in ten or fifteen years, when opportunities may exist for distinction, and lucrative employment may urge the natives to stand by their country. The people have quick perceptive powers, and will soon see where they are well off.

' At present they are not well off, at home. Our mines in Brazil are worked by the Irish, the superior officers are Cornish, but the Irish can throw off their apathy, and do, under proper conditions.'

' And yet you desert them ! '

'God prosper them! Edith, I do. I know the utter futility of attempting to improve matters as an individual.'

'I understand you; tell me more,' said Edith.

'A lost country! my dear, Ireland is lost because she does not know how to manage her resources. They are dormant; she does not create capital, Edith.'

'What does create capital, Gerald?'

'Human labour; and if you ask what gives value to capital, it is man himself. Greece appeared to be over-populated, yet men were considered profitable commodities. Rome imported men also, Edith, when the population seemed overwhelming. Athens had a regular importation of slaves when they were twenty to one of her free men. Even in our great bulwark of freedom, Magna Charta, wrung from John at Runnymede by the Barons, "Vastum hominum et rerum" was regarded an equivalent for injury.

'The serfs of Russia are valued as property. I need not speak of the West Indies or other countries to show that if slave labour be valuable, how much more must be free!

'It would be better for Ireland to cultivate her unreclaimed acres, to invest capital in lucrative trade, and let it increase; hands would soon be found not too many, but too few! Emigration would cease as soon as employment should be found, and Irish murders and disaffection might be stamped out by common sense; and the Celtic trust in destiny would rise to the occasion as it always does elsewhere, where they become hard workers and bread winners, as much as the plodding Anglo-Saxons or the brave Gauls.'

'You should go into Parliament for Ireland, Gerald!'

'Perhaps I may in ten or a dozen years' time. I should only be considered as a revolutionist yet, Edith, by my aristocratic neighbours. I am not inclined to play the part of a patriot, which is ignominious enough as things are at present.'

'I fear you are a deserter, Gerald.'

'I am, my dear, if you like to think so. However, Dublin is undergoing a change for the better; people of all classes are losing the idea that grumbling is the way to success; some have already gone so far in moral courage as to demand respect in virtue of labour, self-reliance, and independence. Some day, Edith, you will like Dublin,—ten years hence.'

'Are you going to Dublin?'

'No, my dear. I have let our place for ten years. I do not mean to go near it.'

'I see you have some plan for me, Gerald. What is it? I do not care, I confess, to go to London.'

'Nor shall you. What do you say to Liverpool for a very short time, only, in fact, till I can purchase such things as must be seen and chosen? I intend to place you and Lilian comfortably at Liverpool for the time it will take me to make arrangements in London, and see my friends the Beaumonts, for I should not like to go away for any long period without visiting them.'

'And they would be disappointed if you did not do so,' said Ella.

'Are you aware that Madame Brinkmann is dead? she made a little halt in her progress to the grave; but it did not surprise me to hear she was gone.'

'She is related to some of the first people at Copenhagen, you know,' said Ella.

'Yes; and the Danish Embassy at Paris paid her every possible respect. Now read this paper carefully. I will come back to you in an hour.'

McLaughlan left her to read.

'Colonization in the Argentine Republic.

'Intelligence has recently been re-

ceived from her Majesty's Chargé d'Affaires
at Buenos Ayres, of the entire failure of
the settlement of Englishmen, which it was
endeavoured to establish in the Argentine
Republic.   This settlement, which at first
consisted of about sixty young men of good
family, who subscribed £150 a piece towards expenses, and which was accom-
panied by a clergyman of the Church of
England and a medical man, it was intended to establish at Fraile Muerio, between Rosario and Cordova.

'Some difficulty, however, having arisen
in obtaining the land contracted for at that
place, it was eventually established at
Rosario.

'According to the prospectus, the colonists were for a certain time to work in
partnership with Mr H. to learn the business, and when they had done so, were to
be put in possession of farms at a price to
be agreed upon beforehand.

'The profits were to be divided each

year, and one half applied to the repayment of the entrance fee, which Mr H.
estimated would be done out of the first
year's profits.

'The colonists arrived at Buenos Ayres
in the spring of last year, and shortly
afterwards proceeded to Rosario, well furnished with farming implements and other
supplies considered necessary for their use.

'It soon, however, became apparent that
they were quite unsuited for the life they
had undertaken. They had not been accustomed to hard labour, and knew nothing
of agriculture.

'On the 27th of July the Chargé d'Affaires at Buenos Ayres reported that several
of the party, including the clergyman and
his family, had returned to England, stating
that they had been brought out under false
pretences.

'Towards the end of September the
colony was visited by Mr Hutchinson, the
British consul of Rosario, who reported

that the colonists did very little work, that almost all the money paid to Mr H., amounting to £10,800, had been spent, and that the colony would probably break up shortly. His anticipation has since been verified.

'On the 11th of November last the Chargé d'Affaires at Buenos Ayres reported that the colony had been abandoned, that Mr H. had disappeared without giving an account of the money he had received, that the colonists, a few of whom linger about Rosario, are ruined, discouraged, and disheartened. Some others are endeavouring to obtain employment on the neighbouring farms, some will try to return to England, others have ventured up the country with the remnants of their limited means, two or three of the most enterprising have started for some imaginary gold fields, in the Sierras of Cordova.

'Thus he says the unfortunate men brought out by Mr H., after losing their capital, find themselves cast adrift penniless in a distant land, ignorant of the language, unprotected, and exposed to every kind of danger.'

Ella read the account, and folded the *Times*.

'Now,' said McLaughlan, 'let us go in and win!'

Ella started,—she did not hear him return, nor know that he was watching her.

'What!' she said, 'go, because they have failed?'

'Yes; they have paved the way for us by their ruin and misfortunes.'

'Tell me how you mean,' said Ella.

'People err constantly in the matter of emigration, and in thinking it is enough to provide transit from the old world to the new. They do not understand the subject, nor know what to do with the emigrants when their destination is reached. We, Edith, with money, a knowledge of Spanish, and means of all sorts, will go out, and receive a new set of emigrants, and provide for their wants.'

'That sounds very nice.'

'There is room and plenty for every-body even without capital, when once some organization has taken place. You will like it, Edith. The Baroness Mc-Laughlan may hold a little court if she likes.'

'Oh no, Gerald.'

'The editor of the *Standard* at Buenos Ayres is a friend of mine. I have a great many friends, both Spanish and English, about Monte Video and Paraguay. Let us go, Edith; it is for your sake as well as my own that I take this step: you would not be quite at ease in England as I wish to see you. Copenhagen has been very well for a time, and you have re-covered yourself now; and, my dear, I could not be idle any longer.'

'I object to nothing, Gerald.'

'You will like your new home and

your assured position. Lilian will be enough to persuade you to leave this : her welfare shall be certain, and with you for chaperone—you see how far-seeing I am.'

'Then is Lilian to go too?'

'Yes; and one object in my journey to London will be to place a goodly sum to accumulate for your baby, in gratitude to you, that she may not only be lovely and accomplished, but wealthy—this—Lilian McLaughlan.'

'She will be very beautiful; but her education?'

'Shall be cared for. She will be with you and with me. She will have nothing to unlearn, and in ten years we can bring her over to finish and polish if we like.'

'We could not leave her in Paris on account of the war, or I might have proposed it,' said Ella.

'That is out of the question, so be happy, for I conclude you would like to have her.'

' Of course I should.'

' Then, Edith, you will aid and abet me ?'

' I will, Gerald. I believe it is for my sake that you go to South America. You think I should not be so happy in England.'

' Nor would you.'

' You are right. With all my determination not to resent former times, it would be difficult for me to meet people whom I used to know. Mr McLaughlan, you understand me better than I do myself; you see my weakness, and where I might be tempted. I have often heard you say there is a great difference between emigrants and immigrants. Which shall I be ?'

' You are my wife. There is all the difference in the world between emigrants and immigrants, so a capitalist should go out first to hold himself ready with supplies to sustain them, and with a scheme ready to employ them; otherwise time is lost and energy is wasted, and it is the hope of the emigrant being dashed to the ground by disappointment which has been the downfall of more projections than one.'

'I will be ready,' said Ella, ' any time you like, to go to Hull. I used to be very impatient. I wanted to see the grass grow; but I am able to wait now, so will remain at Liverpool with Lilian till you have finished all preparations; it is a well arranged scheme.'

McLaughlan was looking out of the window into the broadest street in Copenhagen, one of the widest, indeed, in the world. He repeated something to himself as he gazed on the passing carriages, which ended about 'ten years,' a line from the Blessed Damoselle.

CHAPTER XIII.

THE RING DISPOSED OF.

RUDOLF and Bessie had remained in Paris until they were hastily dismissed by the breaking out of war. It seemed incredible, but the knowledge that Napoleon had left St Cloud, and the after news that the Prince Imperial had received his baptism of fire, induced even stolid English minds to accept facts which they had objected to before.

Bessie had a lovely son and heir to travel with her to England.

Robert met the party in London, and took his brother, Bessie, and his nephew to visit Lord Dunburgher, who received them with so much affectionate warmth, as to surprise Rudolf.

The Duchess of Golden sent for Bessie, and was exceedingly gracious, and quite affable and friendly towards her pretty baby boy.

The young Duke also called upon Rudolf, and promised him shooting; in fact, it was quite evident that Bessie's reception was meant to be from the heart.

Lady Trulybridge claimed her for some days, in order to show her children to her dearest friend, and Bessie suffered herself to be loved and admired very gracefully, for she knew how much pleasure it gave to Rudolf.

Robert had not yet been to the Grange.

' I said I would never go to Beaumont Grange without Bessie,' was the excuse which he made to himself; nor did he go there till he went to meet McLaughlan some time later.

It was with much contentment that

McLaughlan drove up to Beaumont Grange, to be received there by Rudolf and Bessie and the baby son, who was duly presented, with—

'Mr McLaughlan, we have named him after you!'

'Have you, Mrs Beaumont? you do me too much honour.'

'Yes; he is "Robert McLaughlan." Robert and you are his godfathers if you please, but Robert said you would not like him to have your other name; indeed, he did not tell us what it is, and as you always sign your letters McLaughlan only, it seems quite natural, and I think "Robert McLaughlan Beaumont" is a very nice name,' said Bessie.

'So do I.' And McLaughlan kissed the little boy, and took him in his great, strong arms, and nursed him, walking up and down the room, whilst his mother, glad to watch the large, square man caressing her child, heard from him all he chose to tell her concerning Lilian, and how he had left Ella at Liverpool ready to sail by the 'Patagonia' when he had transacted his business in London.

'Robert is to come this evening to see you,' Bessie said; 'he has not yet been here, but Rudolf wrote for him to come and meet you, and he is coming.'

'I am very glad.'

'I suppose you heard of the weddings?'

'No; tell me.'

'Lord Dunburgher's two daughters were married at the same time, one to Lord Cranbourne, the other to Major Harris, for whom they waited; but Robert was kept very busy by Lord Dunburgher.'

'Well, as he is coming here I need not go to him, so I may play with my namesake as long as I like.'

'Mr McLaughlan,' Bessie said after a pause, ' I cannot help hoping there may be a third wedding soon.'

'Whose do you wish it to be?'

' Robert Beaumont to Lady Susan
Goldenisle. I may tell you that she has
loved him ever since she was quite a child.
Robert must have met her, I think, very
often since he has been at Lord Dunburgher's. I do so hope he has begun to
know her value.'

' What if I were to offer him congratulations ? '

' I hardly know what should be done;
but Susan is so fond of him,—she has never
liked any one else. She was very delicate
for a long time, and I found out how much
she cared for Robert Beaumont. After
she came from the West Indies they took
her out, and to Florence, for one winter,
another time to Rome; but she is still unmarried, and I know Robert Beaumont is
all the world to her.'

' Is Robert aware of it ? '

' I do not know; I suppose not; but
she is so very nice, Mr McLaughlan. I am
sure she would make him happy, and I

know the Duchess will approve, and the Duke likes Robert very much. The young Duke has turned out so nicely: he is a good husband, an excellent landlord, and is very kind to his sisters.'

'You esteem him,—that is enough.'

'Mr McLaughlan,' continued Bessie, rising to pace with him up and down the drawing-room, for the little one had fallen asleep in the comfortable arms, 'if you can say anything to Robert which may accelerate this affair I shall be so happy, and you can do anything you will.'

'But has he proposed, Mrs Beaumont?'

'I hardly know: he has not been here, and I have not liked to ask anything. He has been at Oxford, do you know this? and is now ready for Lord Bluebook's chaplaincy; but I think if he had proposed I should have heard of it, for I am certain Susan could not refuse him.'

'Well, it is something to be sure he will be accepted.'

Robert came. It was dinner-time immediately after his arrival, and some of the neighbouring gentry had been invited to meet the Baron and Robert Beaumont, so they had to give way for that evening to the requirements of society.

Next day McLaughlan said to Bessie, 'Mrs Beaumont, I asked Robert what Lady Susan Goldenisle is like, and he replied, "Like a fair tall lily."'

'So she is, exactly,' said Bessie.

'I am to go with him to-morrow to see her, so I rather think, Mrs Beaumont, that matters are pretty much in the sort of condition that you wish.'

'You are a true friend, Mr McLaughlan. I know you will like Susan very much, and agree with me that she is worthy of Robert.'

It was not without pain that McLaughlan took leave of Beaumont Grange, though he heartily rejoiced that he had seen Rudolf and Bessie so happily settled there.

McLaughlan and Robert spent days in London together, which proved the friendship already cemented between them; indeed, Robert was quite low and out of spirits as the moment for departure drew near.

At last he returned to the Grange, just in time for dinner, and could say very little, and retired early. He had been to Liverpool, and had seen McLaughlan and his wife and Lilian sail by one of the Brazil and River Plate mail steamers.

Gradually he began to talk of him and of his projects.

'McLaughlan is the right man to go out,' he said, 'and organize a scheme from which gain, and not ruin, will be the result. There is a natural current from the old country to the newer lands, but such men are wanted as Mr McLaughlan to arrange for the new comers.'

Rudolf asked for all sorts of particulars, but we need not repeat all that Robert told him.

'Bessie,' Robert said, 'I ought to tell you that Lord Dunburgher has made me his heir. His daughters are amply provided for, and are also married, so Lord Dunburgher says he is free to do as he likes. It was he who got me Lord Bluebook's chaplaincy; indeed, McLaughlan and he seem to have settled everything.'

Bessie looked pleased. Her husband asked, 'What is the chaplaincy? Is it to be in the army?'

'I hardly know yet; I feel so much the parting with McLaughlan.'

'What did he do with the ring?'

'The ring?' said Robert with a little flush. 'I think the ring has done all the good it could do, for, Bessie, Lady Susan Goldenisle has consented to be mine.'

Bessie crossed the room and kissed him. Rudolf wrung his hand in silence.

Robert walked up and down for some moments, just as McLaughlan had done. Rudolf broke the reverie by stating,

' You cannot be Lord Dunburgher ! '

'No; but I am to have the name tacked on to Beaumont. I do not care now; perhaps the Duchess may like it better.'

' Oh, Robert ! '

' She may, Bessie, prefer Beaumont Dunburgher to plain Robert Beaumont.'

' Did she tell you so ? '

She has told me very little as yet. It was McLaughlan, whom Susan likes very much, who induced me to try my fate; but I could not ask her, so I wrote to her, and she has accepted me to-day.'

' I am so very very glad.'

' I shall hear what Susan says; perhaps, as she likes McLaughlan too, we may follow him to Rosario.'

' And where is the ring ? '

' He brought it to me the day after we had both been to see Lady Susan.' He said, " I think it has done all its work now," so, with his great heart, he made it a donation to the sick and wounded in the war; that is, he gave me fifty pounds for it, which was sent to the fund.'

'What a nice thing to do! So you have it still, Robert?'

'The Scandinavian Ring itself is deposited in the museum at Daneton, which our friend McLaughlan founded some time ago as a memorial to poor Mr Sutton. He has since sent a thousand pounds to Daneton—'

Robert stopped; his voice faltered. Rudolf's blue eyes glistened as he left the room.

Bessie, with her loving smile, said, 'The ring has done all the good it could. I only hope Mr McLaughlan has found his reward.'

'I think he has; he deserves it as no other man on earth, and I think Ella Storton appreciates her good fortune.'

It was early in autumn, beautiful and bright, but in the wide room at Beaumont Grange a fire had been lighted.

Robert went towards it, and without disguising it from Bessie, he opened the locket which he wore, and burnt a bit of dried pink flower, saying,

' Susan is very fond of you, Bessie ! '

Bessie answered with a prayer.

' Whilst at Copenhagen McLaughlan began to turn our affairs into a romance.'

' How can we finish it, Robert ? '

' I cannot say. Susan may wish for Lord Bluebook's chaplaincy : I for Rosario. It may come to be Ireland " after ten years," as McLaughlan says. We all owe a good deal to the Scandinavian Ring : at present it is a story without an end.'

THE END.

JOHN CHILDS AND SON, PRINTERS.

www.ingramcontent.com/pod-product-compliance
Lightning Source LLC
Chambersburg PA
CBHW020851020726
47497CB00005B/1362